THE UPRISING

Don Orteva, turned to the few men who remained near him,
"Stand by me, my brave lads!" he cried. And advancing toward
Martinez, "Seize that officer!" he exclaimed.

"Death to the commander!" replied Martinez. * * * *

The bullet from Don Orteva's pistol was lost in space. The
captain crossed swords with the lieutenant, but, overwhelmed by
numbers and severely wounded, he was borne to the deck.—Page 164.

EARLY STORIES
OF
JULES VERNE

BY

JULES VERNE

Fredonia Books
Amsterdam, The Netherlands

Early Stories of Jules Verne

by
Jules Verne

ISBN: 1-4101-0026-X

Fredonia Books
Amsterdam, The Netherlands
http://www.fredoniabooks.com

and without imagination man is nothing; for all greatness is but a phase of imagination. It is the creative force of the world. Under Verne's guidance his readers travel in every land, examine every mode of life and labor, view all the strangest wonders of the universe.

The educators of youth have been swift to recognize the high value of the masterworks of this mighty magician. His simpler tales are used as text-books in our American schools, both in French and English. And the conscience of the moralist can here approve the eager pleasure of the reader, and bid youth continue to bask in this glorious light of wonder and adventure. There is not an evil nor uncleanly line in all the volumes. Never did anyone lay aside one of Verne's books without being a better, broader, nobler human being because of their perusal.

Surely the time is ripe when a definitive edition of the master's works should be given to American readers. Jules Verne died in 1905; and, though he left behind him in the hands of his Paris publishers an unusually large number of unissued works, the last of these has now been given to the public. Moreover we can now estimate his work calmly, unconfused by the tumultuous and very varying opinions pronounced upon it by the French critics of his own day.

JULES VERNE

HE expander of horizons," is what a noted critic called Jules Verne. He was the prophet, the foreseer and foreteller of our great mechanical age. He belongs to-day not to France, but to the world. Widely as his works have been read in his own country, their popularity has been yet wider in America and England. Much as he has been honored at home, even higher glory has been accorded him, we are told, in far Japan. His books have been translated not only into all the usual languages, but into Hebrew, Japanese, Polish and even Arabic.

Verne was a universal teacher, both of youth and age. From him the whole world garnered knowledge without effort; for all listened with pleasure while he spun his tales. He was a supreme master of imagination,

Jules Verne

JULES VERNE

Their obituary reviews of
his work differed widely as to
its value. On the one hand,
the noted critic, Morel, in the
authoritative "Nouvelle Re-
vue" declared Verne to be the
leading educator and perhaps
the most read author of the
new twentieth century. At the
other extreme were the un-
signed assaults of those who
could only make a mock of
what was too open and too honest for them to comprehend.

Verne's Home

Verne was no intricate analyst, elaborating such
subtleties of thought and ethics as only subtle folk
can understand. He spoke for the great mass of
men, giving them such tales as they could follow,
upholding always such a standard of courage and
virtue, simple and high, as each of us can honor for
himself and be glad to set before his children.

It is not only "boy's literature" that began with
Verne. One might almost say that man's literature, the story that appeals to the business man,
the practical man, began then also. The great
French "Encyclopédie Universelle" sums up his
books by saying, "They instruct a little, entertain
much, and overflow with life."

JULES VERNE

Jules Verne was the establisher of a new species of story-telling, that which interweaves the most stupendous wonders of science with the simplest facts of human life. Our own Edgar Allen Poe had pointed the way; and Verne was ever eager to acknowledge his indebtedness to the earlier master. But Poe died; and it was Verne who went on in book after book, fascinating his readers with cleverly devised mysteries, instructing and astonishing them with the new discoveries of science, inspiring them with the splendor of man's destiny. When, as far back as 1872, his early works were "crowned" by the French Academy, its Perpetual Secretary, M. Patin, said in his official address, "The well-worn wonders of fairyland are here replaced by a new and more marvelous world, created from the most recent ideas of science."

More noteworthy still is Verne's position as the true, the astonishingly true, prophet of the discoveries and inventions that were to come. He was far more than the mere creator of that sort of scientific fairyland of which Secretary Patin spoke, and with which so many later writers, Wells, Haggard and Sir Conan Doyle, have since delighted us. He himself once keenly contrasted his own methods with those of Wells, the man he most admired among his many followers. Wells, he pointed out, looked centuries ahead and out of pure imagination embodied the unknowable that some day might perchance appear. "While I," said Verne, "base my inventions on a groundwork of actual fact." He illustrated this by instancing his submarine, the Nautilus. "This," said he, "when carefully considered, is a submarine mechanism about which there is nothing wholly extraordinary, nor beyond the bounds of actual scientific knowledge. It rises and sinks by perfectly well-known processes. . . . Its motive force even is no secret; the only point at which I have called in the aid of imagination is in the application of this force, and here I have purposely left a blank, for the reader to form his own conclusion, a mere technical hiatus."

So it comes that Verne's prophecies already spring to realization on every side. He foresaw and in his vivid way described not only the submarine, but also, in his "Steam-house," the automobile, in his "Robur the Conqueror," the aeroplane. Navigable balloons, huge aerial machines heavier than air, the telephone, moving pavements, stimulation by oxygen, compressed air, compressed food, all were existant among his clear-sighted visions. And to-day as we read those even bolder prophecies, accounts that excited only the laughter of his earlier critics, it is with ever-increasing wonder as to which will next come true.

His influence has been tremendous, not only

upon story-telling, but upon life. One French commentator cries with profound admiration that Verne "wholly changed the conversation of the drawing-rooms." Another, with perhaps broader understanding, declares that he revolutionized the thought of the young men of his earlier days. "He taught us that the forces of nature, enemies to man in his ignorance, stood ready to be our servants once we had learned to master and control them."

For a writer so much read, Jules Verne has been very little talked about. His personality became submerged in his work. Moreover he was not a Parisian, not a member of the mutual admiration club which exists perforce in every artistic center, where the same little circle of able men constantly meeting, and writing one about the other, impress all their names upon the public. Verne early withdrew from the turmoil and clamor of the French capital to dwell in peace at Amiens. To ignore Paris, to withdraw deliberately from its already

won caresses! Could any crime have been more heinous in Parisian eyes? It explains the rancor of at least some of the French critics in their attitude toward our author.

Known thus only through his books, yet by them known

Verne's Tower Workroom

so universally, Verne has already become a myth. Legends have gathered around his form. In Germany writers have ponderously explained —and believed—that he was not a Frenchman at all, but a Jew, a native of Russian Poland. They gave him a birthplace, in the town of Plock, and a name, Olshewitz, of which Vergne or Verne was

The Saint Michel

only a French translation, since both words mean the alder tree. In Italy about 1886 the report became widespread that he was dead, or rather that he had never lived, that he was only a name used in common by an entire syndicate of authors, who contributed their best works and best efforts to popularize the series of books whose profits they shared in common. Even in France itself men learned to say, for the sake of the antithesis, that this, the greatest of all writers of travel, had gained all his knowledge out of books and never himself had traveled beyond Amiens.

Lest to American readers also, the man, the truly lovable man, Verne, should become wholly lost behind his books, let us make brief record of him here. He was born in Nantes, the chief city of

Brittany, on February 8, 1828. His father was a lawyer in good circumstances, and Jules' early training was also for the law. The chief pleasure of his youth lay in a battered old sailing boat, in which he and his brother Paul, taking turns at being captain, played all the stories of the sea, and explored every reach of the River Loire, even down to the mighty ocean. That sloop still echoes through his every book.

Sent to Paris to complete his studies, Jules soon drifted away from the law. He became part and parcel of all the Bohemian life of Paris, a student, artist, author, poet, clerking all day that he might live and dream and scribble all the night. A typical "son of the boulevards," they called him in those days. He became a close friend of the younger Dumas, and was introduced to his friend's yet more celebrated father, the Alexander Dumas of romance. The father guided and advised him; the son collaborated with him in his first literary success—if literary it can be called—a little one act comedy in verse, "Broken Straws," produced at the "Gymnase" in 1850. Then came librettos for comic operas, short stories for little-known story papers; and young Verne was fairly launched upon a career of authorship.

In 1857 he journeyed eighty miles to Amiens, so the story is told, to act as best man at the wedding of a friend. Before this he had long vowed himself to a single life. Art, he said, and woman were two different mistresses, and no man could truly serve both. But at Amiens he arrived late, the bridal party was already gone, and no one was left to receive the laggard but a sister of the bride, a young widow who had stayed at home to keep from casting her gloom upon the festivity. Within the hour both Jules and the young widow, Mme. de Vianne, had abandoned all their former views, and recognized each other as life companions. This sounds like another legend; but it seems well vouched for. Verne married Mme. de Vianne within the year.

In 1860 or shortly after, Verne met the one other person who was most to influence his life, the great Parisian publisher, Hetzel, who had issued the works of Hugo, of Georges Sand, and of DeMusset. Hetzel, who had been in exile in Brussels, returned to Paris in 1860: and our author soon began writing for him. The two became warm friends.

Verne's first full length novel or story was issued by Hetzel in 1863. This epoch-making book was "Five Weeks in a Balloon." In it the young author attained for the first time his characteristic vein of explorations into unknown regions, intermingling the new science with adventures and heroism as old as man.

The book was a tremendous success. The whole world read, and was delighted. Hetzel started a "Magazine of Education and Recreation," which was chiefly supported by Verne's writings. Author

Verne's Tombstone

and publisher made a twenty year contract, under which Verne was to produce two books a year; and being thus assured of financial independence, Verne in 1870 withdrew with his wife to her native Amiens. There he lived in quietude for over thirty-five years, until his death.

The legend that he never quitted Amiens at all is, however, false. Twice at least he journeyed to the British Isles, and once, though before his retirement to Amiens, to America and once to Scandinavia. Moreover his youthful love for sailing clung to him. In a little ten ton boat, he cruised much in summer along the French coast; and later in life he owned a handsome hundred foot steam yacht, the "Saint Michel," in which he visited Mediterranean Africa, Malta and much of the European coast.

Chiefly, however, Verne's later life was devoted to his books, and to the civic world of Amiens. He was a member of the town council, an active and earnest member, who won the devoted regard of his fellow townsmen.

He and the grand cathedral of Amiens were the city's twin celebrities, their pictures standing side by side in shop-windows and decorating postal cards. The Verne homestead was on one of the principal boulevards, a handsome house with, at its rear, a tower, the topmost room of which formed a secluded den where the writer worked.

In this tower room, he continued steadily producing his stories. As far back as 1872 he had been a candidate for the celebrated French Academy, with strong chances of election. But the Academy, while it crowned his individual books, refused membership to their author, though after that first candidacy he in the course of his later life watched the entire membership of the Academy pass and be renewed twice over. His friends, especially his Amiens townfolk, declared that his exclusion was due to Parisian jealousy, and that the Academy lost far more honor than the author by ignoring him. "Paris," said one of them, "had nothing worthy of this great man. He sought a place for work; Paris offers its great men only lounging places."

CONTENTS

INTRODUCTION

"A Drama in the Air," was, as Verne himself tells us, his first published story. It appeared soon after 1850 in a little-known local magazine called the "Musée des Familles." The tale, though somewhat amateurish, is very characteristic of the master's later style. In it we can see, as it were, the germ of all that was to follow, the interest in the new advances of science, the dramatic story, the carefully collected knowledge of the past, the infusion of instruction amid the excitement of the tale.

Similarly we find "A Winter in the Ice" to be a not unworthy predecessor of "The Adventures of Captain Hatteras" and all the author's other great books of adventure in the frozen world. Here, at the first attempt, a vigorous and impressive story introduces us to the northland, thoroughly understood, accurately described, vividly appreciated and pictured forth in its terror and its mystery.

"The Pearl of Lima" opens the way to all those stories of later novelists wherein some ancient kingly race, some forgotten civilization of Africa or America, reasserts itself in the person of some spectacular descendant, tragically matching its obscure and half-demoniac powers against the might of the modern world. "The Mutineers" inaugurates our author's favorite geographical device. It describes a remarkable and little-known country by having the characters of the story travel over it on some anxious errand, tracing their progress step by step.

Thus, of these five early tales, "The Watch's Soul" is the only one differing sharply from Verne's later work. It is allegorical, supernatural, depending not upon the scientific marvels of the material world, but upon the direct interposition of supernal powers.

I

A Drama in the Air

I N the month of September, 185—, I arrived at Frankfort-on-the-Main. My passage through the principal German cities had been brilliantly marked by balloon ascents; but as yet no German had accompanied me in my car, and the fine experiments made at Paris by MM. Greene, Eugene Godard, and Poitevin had not tempted the grave Teutons to essay aerial voyages.

But scarcely had the news of my approaching ascent spread through Frankfort, than three of the principal citizens begged the favor of being allowed to ascend with me. Two days afterwards we were to start from the Place de la Comédie. I began at once to get my balloon ready. It was of silk, prepared with gutta percha; and its volume, which was three thousand cubic yards, enabled it to ascend to the loftiest heights.

The day of the ascent was that of the great September fair, which attracts so many people to Frankfort. Lighting gas, of perfect quality and great lifting power, had been furnished me, and about eleven o'clock the balloon was filled; but only three-quarters filled,—an indispensable precaution, for, as one rises, the atmosphere diminishes in density, and the fluid enclosed within the balloon, acquiring more elasticity, might burst its sides. My calculations told me exactly the quantity of gas necessary to carry up my companions and myself.

We were to start at noon. The impatient crowd which pressed around the enclosed square, overflowing into the contiguous streets, and covering the houses from the ground-floor to the slated gables, presented a striking scene.

I carried three hundred pounds of ballast in bags; the car, quite round, four feet in diameter, was comfortably arranged; the hempen cords which supported it stretched symmetrically over the upper hemisphere of the balloon; the

3

compass was in place, the barometer suspended in the circle which united the supporting cords, and the anchor put in order. All was now ready for the ascent.

Among those who pressed around the enclosure, I remarked a young man with a pale face and agitated features. The sight of him impressed me. He was an eager spectator of my ascents, whom I had already met in several German cities. With an uneasy air, he closely watched the curious machine, as it lay motionless a few feet above the ground; and he remained silent among those about him.

Twelve o'clock came. The moment had arrived, but my traveling companions did not appear.

I sent to their houses, and learnt that one had left for Hamburg, another for Vienna, and the third for London. Their courage had failed them at undertaking one of those excursions which, thanks to the improvement in aeronautics are free from all danger. As they formed, in some sort, a part of the programme of the day, the fear had seized them that they might be forced to execute it faithfully, and they had fled far from the scene at the instant when the balloon was being filled. Their heroism was evidently in inverse ratio to their speed—in decamping.

The multitude, half deceived, showed not a little ill humor. I did not hesitate to ascend alone. In order to re-establish the equilibrium between the specific gravity of the balloon and the weight which had thus proved wanting, I replaced my companions by more sacks of sand, and got into the car. The twelve men who held the balloon by twelve cords, let these slip a little between their fingers, and the balloon rose several feet higher. There was not a breath of wind, and the atmosphere was so laden that it seemed to forbid the ascent.

" Is everything ready? " I cried.

The men put themselves in readiness. A last glance told me that I might go. " Attention! "

There was a movement in the crowd, which seemed to be invading the enclosure.

" Let go! "

The balloon rose slowly, but I experienced a shock which threw me to the bottom of the car.

When I got up, I found myself face to face with an unexpected fellow-voyager,—the pale young man.

"Monsieur, I salute you," said he, with utmost coolness.

"By what right——"

"Am I here? By the right which the impossibility of your getting rid of me confers."

I was amazed! His calmness put me out of countenance, and I had nothing to reply. I looked at the intruder but he took no notice of my astonishment.

"Does my weight disarrange your equilibrium, monsieur?" he asked. "You will permit me—" and without waiting consent, he picked up two bags and threw them into space.

"Monsieur," said I, taking the only course now possible, "you have come; very well, you will remain; but to me alone belongs the management of the balloon."

"Monsieur," said he, "your urbanity is French all over: it comes from my own country. I morally press the hand you refuse me. Make all precautions, and act as seems best to you. I will wait till you have done——"

"For what?"

"To talk with you."

The barometer had fallen to twenty-six inches. We were nearly six hundred yards above the city; but nothing betrayed the horizontal displacement of the balloon, for the mass of air in which it is enclosed goes forward with it. A sort of confused glow enveloped the objects spread out under us, and fortunately obscured their outline.

I examined my companion afresh. He was a man of thirty years, simply clad. The sharpness of his features betrayed an indomitable energy, and he seemed very muscular. Indifferent to the astonishment he created, he remained motionless, trying in the meantime to distinguish the objects below us.

"Miserable mist!" said he, after a few moments.

I did not reply.

"You owe me a grudge?" he went on. "Bah! I could not pay for my journey, and it was necessary to take you by surprise."

"Nobody asks you to descend, monsieur!"

"Eh, do you not know, then, that the same thing happened to the Counts of Laurencin and Dampierre, when they ascended at Lyons, on the 15th of January, 1784? A young merchant, named Fontaine, scaled the gallery, at the risk of capsizing the machine. He accomplished the journey, and nobody died of it!"

"Once on the ground, we will have an explanation," replied I, piqued at the light tone in which he spoke.

"Bah! Do not let us think of our return."

"Do you think, then, I shall not hasten to descend?"

"Descend!" said he, in surprise. "Descend? Let us begin by first ascending."

And before I could prevent it, two more bags had been thrown out of the car, without even having been emptied.

"Monsieur!" cried I, in a rage.

"I know your ability," replied the unknown quietly, "and your fine ascents are famous. But if Experience is the sister of Practice, she is also a cousin of Theory, and I have studied the aerial art long. It has got into my head!" he added sadly, falling into a silent reverie.

The balloon, having risen some distance farther, now become stationary. The unknown consulted the barometer and said, "Here we are, at eight hundred yards. Men are like insects. See! I think we should always contemplate them from this height, to judge correctly of their proportions. The Place de la Comédie is transformed into an immense ant-hill. Observe the crowd which is gathered on the quays; and the mountains also get smaller and smaller. We are over the Cathedral. The Main is only a line, cutting the city in two, and the bridge seems a thread thrown between the two banks of the river."

The atmosphere became somewhat chilly.

"There is nothing I would not do for you, my host," said the unknown. "If you are cold, I will take off my coat and lend it to you."

"Thanks," said I dryly.

"Bah! Necessity makes law. Give me your hand. I am your fellow-countryman; you will learn something in my company, and my conversation will indemnify you for the trouble I have given you."

I sat down, without replying, at the opposite extremity of the car. The young man drew a voluminous manuscript from his coat. It was an essay on ballooning.

"I possess," said he, "the most curious collection of engravings and caricatures extant concerning aerial manias. How people admired and scoffed at the same time at this precious discovery! We are happily no longer in the age in which Montgolfier tried to make artificial clouds with steam, or a gas having electrical properties, produced by the combustion of moist straw and chopped-up-wool."

"Do you wish to depreciate the talent of the inventors?" I asked, for I had resolved to enter into the adventure. "Was it not good to have proved by experience the possibility of rising in the air?"

"Ah, monsieur, who denies the glory of the first aerial navigators? It required immense courage to rise by means of those frail envelopes which only contained heated air. But I ask you, has the aerial science made great progress since Blanchard's ascensions, that is, since nearly a century ago? Look here, monsieur."

The unknown took an engraving from his portfolio.

"Here," said he, "is the first aerial voyage undertaken by Pilâtre des Rosiers and the Marquis d'Arlandes, four months after the discovery of balloons. Louis XVI. refused to consent to the venture, and two men who were condemned to death were the first to attempt the aerial ascent. Pilâtre des Rosiers became indignant at this injustice, and, by means of intrigues, obtained permission to make the experiment. The car, which renders the management easy, had not then been invented, and a circular gallery was placed around the lower and contracted part of the Montgolfier balloon. The two aeronauts must then remain motionless at each extremity of this gallery, for the moist straw which filled it forbade them all motion. A chafing-dish with fire was suspended below the orifice of the balloon; when the aeronauts wished to rise, they threw straw upon this brazier, at the risk of setting fire to the balloon, and the air, more heated, gave it fresh ascending power. The two bold travelers rose, on the 21st of November, 1783, from the Muette Gardens, which the dauphin had put at their disposal. The balloon went up majestically, passed over the Isle of Swans, crossed the Seine at the Conference barrier, and, drifting between the dome of the Invalids and the Military School, approached the Church of Saint Sulpice. Then the aeronauts added to the fire, crossed the Boulevard, and descended beyond the Enfer barrier. As it touched the soil, the balloon collapsed, and for a few moments buried Pilâtre des Rosiers under its folds."

"Unlucky augury," I said, interested in the story, which affected me nearly.

"An augury of the catastrophe which was later to cost this unfortunate man his life," replied the unknown sadly. "Have you never experienced anything like it?"

"Never."

"Bah! Misfortunes sometimes occur unforeshadowed!" added my companion. He then remained silent.

We were drifting southward, and Frankfort had already passed from beneath us.

"Perhaps we shall have a storm," said the young man.

"We shall descend before that," I replied.

"Better to ascend. We shall escape it more surely." And two more bags of sand were hurled into space.

The balloon rose rapidly, and stopped at twelve hundred yards. I became colder; and yet the sun's rays, falling upon the surface, expanded the gas within, and gave it a greater ascending force.

"Fear nothing," said the unknown. "We have still three thousand five hundred fathoms of breathing air. Besides, do not trouble yourself about what I do."

I would have risen, but a vigorous hand held me to my seat. "Your name?" I asked.

"My name? What matters it to you?"

"I demand your name!"

"My name is Erostratus or Empedocles, whichever you choose!"

This reply was far from reassuring. The unknown, besides, talked with such strange coolness that I anxiously asked myself whom I had to deal with.

"Monsieur," he continued, "nothing original has been imagined since the physicist Charles. Four months after the discovery of balloons, this man had invented the valve which permits the gas to escape when the balloon is too full, or when you wish to descend; the car, which aids the management of the machine; the netting, which holds the envelope of the balloon, and divides the weight over its whole surface; the ballast, which enables you to ascend, and to choose the place of your landing; the india-rubber coating, which renders the tissue impermeable; the barometer, which shows the height attained. Lastly, Charles used hydrogen, which, fourteen times lighter than air, permits you to penetrate to the highest atmospheric regions, and does not expose you to the dangers of a combustion in the air. On the 1st of December, 1783, three hundred thousand spectators were crowded around the Tuilleries. Charles rose, and the soldiers presented arms to him. He traveled nine leagues in the air, conducting his balloon with an ability not surpassed by modern aeronauts. The king awarded him a pension of two thousand livres; for then they encouraged new inventions."

The unknown now seemed to be under the influence of considerable agitation.

" See, there is Darmstadt," said he, leaning over the car. " Do you perceive the château? Not very distinctly, eh? What would you have? The heat of the storm makes the outline of objects waver, and you must have a skilled eye to recognize localities."

" Are you certain it is Darmstadt? " I asked

" I am sure of it. We are now six leagues from Frankfort."

" Then we must descend."

" Descend! You would not go down on the steeples," said the unknown, with a chuckle.

" No, but in the surburbs of the city."

" Well, let us avoid the steeples! "

So speaking, my companion seized some bags of ballast. I hastened to prevent him; but he overthrew me with one hand, and the unballasted balloon ascended to two thousand yards.

" Rest easy," said he, " and do not forget that Brioschi, Biot, Gay-Lussac, Bixio, and Barral ascended to still greater heights to make their scientific experiments."

" Monsieur, we must descend," I resumed, trying to persuade him by gentleness. " The storm is gathering around us. It would be more prudent——"

" Bah! We will mount higher than the storm, and then we shall no longer fear it! " cried my companion. " What is nobler than to overlook the clouds which oppress the earth? Is it not an honor thus to navigate on aerial billows? The greatest men have traveled as we are doing. The Marchioness and Countees de Montalembert, the Countess of Podenas, Mademoiselle la Garde, the Marquis de Montalembert, rose from the Faubourg Saint-Antoine for these

unknown regions, and the Duke de Chartres exhibited much
skill and presence of mind in his ascent on the 15th of July,
174. At Lyons, the Counts of Laurencin and Dampierre;
at Nantes, M. de Luynes; at Bordeaux, D'Arbelet des
Granges; in Italy, the Chevalier Andreani; in our own time,
the Duke of Brunswick,—have all left traces of their glory
in the air. To equal these great personages, we must penetrate still higher than they into the celestial depths! To
approach the infinite is to comprehend it!"

The rarefaction of the air was fast expanding the hydrogen in the balloon, and I saw its lower part, purposely left
empty, swell out, so that it was absolutely necessary to open
the valve; but my companion did not seem to intend that I
should manage the balloon as I wished. I then resolved
to pull the valve-cord secretly, as he was excitedly talking;
for I feared to guess with whom I had to deal. It would
have been too horrible! It was nearly a quarter before one.
We had been gone forty minutes from Frankfort; heavy
clouds were coming against the wind from the south, and
seemed about to burst upon us.

"Have you lost all hope of succeeding in your project?"
I asked with anxious interest.

"All hope!" exclaimed the unknown in a low voice.
"Wounded by slights and caricatures, these asses' kicks have
finished me! It is the eternal punishment reserved for in-
novators! Look at these caricatures of all periods, of which
my portfolio is full."

While my companion was fumbling with his papers, I
had seized the valve-cord without his perceiving it. I
feared, however, that he might hear the hissing noise, like a
water-course, which the gas makes in escaping.

"How many jokes were made about the Abbé Miolan!
said he. "He was to go up with Janninet and Bredin.
During the filling their ballon caught fire, and the ignorant
populace tore it in pieces! Then this caricature of 'curious
animals' appeared, giving each of them a punning nick-
name."

I pulled the valve-cord, and the barometer began to ascend. It was time. Some far-off rumblings were heard in
the south.

"Here is another engraving," resumed the unknown, not
suspecting what I was doing. "It is an immense balloon

carrying a ship, strong castles, houses, and so on. The caricaturists did not suspect that their follies would one day become truths. It is complete, this large vessel. On the left is its helm, with the pilot's box; at the prow are pleasure-houses, an immense organ, and a cannon to call the attention of the inhabitants of the earth or the moon; above the poop there are the observatory and the balloon long-boat; in the equatorial circle, the army barrack; on the left, the funnel; then the upper galleries for promenading, sails, pinions; below, the cafés and general storehouse. Observe this pompous announcement: 'Invented for the happiness of the human race, this globe will depart at once for the ports of the Levant, and on its return the programme of its voyages to the two poles and the extreme west will be announced. No one need furnish himself with anything; everything is foreseen, and all will prosper. Thus pleasure will be the soul of the aerial company.' All this provoked laughter; but before long, if I am not cut off, they will see it all realized."

We were visibly descending. He did not perceive it!

"This kind of 'game at balloons,'" he resumed, spreading out before me some of the engravings of his valuable collection, "this game contains the entire history of the aerostatic art. It is used by elevated minds, and displayed with dice and counters, with whatever stakes you like, to be paid or received according to where the player arrives."

"Why," said I, "you seem to have studied the science of aerostation profoundly."

"Yes, monsieur, yes! From Phaeton, Icarus, Architas, I have searched for, examined, learnt everything. I could render immense services to the world in this art, if God granted me life. But that will not be!"

"Why?"

"Because my name is Empedocles, or Erostratus."

Meanwhile, the balloon was happily approaching the earth; but when one is falling, the danger is as great at a hundred feet as at five thousand.

"Do you recall the battle of Fleurus?" resumed my companion, whose face became more and more animated. "It was at that battle that Contello, by order of the Government, organized a company of ballonists. At the siege of Manbenge General Jourdan derived so much service from this new method of observation that Contello ascended twice a day with the general himself. The communications between the aeronaut and his agents who held the balloon were made by means of small white, red, and yellow flags. Often the gun and cannon shot were directed upon the balloon when he ascended, but without result. Where General Jourdan was perparing to invest Charleroi, Contello went in the vicinity, ascended from the plain of Jumet, and continued his observations for seven or eight hours with General Morlot, and this no doubt aided in giving us the victory of Fleurus. General Jourdan publicly acknowledged the help which the aeronautical observations had afforded him. Well, despite the services rendered on that occasion and during the Belgian campaign, the year which had seen the beginning of the military career of balloons saw also its end. The school of Meudon, founded by the Government, was closed by Buonaparte on his return from Egypt. And now, what can you expect from the new-born infant? as Franklin said. The infant was born alive; it should not be stifled!"

The unknown bowed his head in his hands for some moments; then rousing himself, he said, "Despite my prohibition, monsieur, you have opened the valve."

I dropped the cord.

"Happily," he resumed, "we have still three hundred pounds of ballast."

"What is your purpose?" said I.

"Have you ever crossed the seas?" he asked.

I turned pale.

"It is unfortunate," he went on, "that we are being driven towards the Adriatic. That is only a stream; but higher up we may find other currents."

And, without taking any notice of me, he threw over several bags of sand; then, in a menacing voice, he said, "I let you open the valve because the expanding gas threatened to burst the balloon; but do not do it again!"

Then he went on, "You remember the voyage of Blanchard and Jeffries from Dover to Calais? It was magnificent! On the 7th of January, 1785, there being a north-west wind, their balloon was inflated with gas on the Dover coast. A mistake of equilibrium, just as they were ascending, forced them to throw out their ballast so that they might not go down again, and they only kept thirty pounds. It was too little; for, as the wind did not freshen, they only advanced very slowly towards the French coast. Besides, the permeability of the tissue served to reduce the inflation little by little, and in an hour and a half the aeronauts perceived that they were descending.

" ' What shall we do?' said Jeffries.

" ' We are only one quarter of the way over,' replied Blanchard, ' and very low down. On rising, we shall perhaps meet more favorable winds.'

" ' Let us throw out the rest of the sand.'

" The balloon acquired some ascending force, but it soon began to descend again. Towards the middle of the transit the aeronauts threw over their books and tools. A quarter of an hour after, Blanchard said to Jeffries, ' The barometer?'

" ' It is going up! We are lost, and yet there is the French coast.'

" A loud noise was heard.

" ' Has the balloon burst?' asked Jeffries.

" ' No. The loss of the gas has reduced the inflation of the lower part of the balloon. But we are still descending. We are lost! Out with everything useless!'

" Provisions, oars, and rudder were thrown into the sea. The aeronauts were only one hundred yards high.

" ' We are going up again,' said the doctor.

" ' No. It is the spurt caused by the diminution of the weight, and not a ship in sight, not a bark on the horizon! To the sea with our clothing!'

" The unfortunates stripped themselves, but the balloon continued to descend.

" ' Blanchard,' said Jeffries, ' you should have made this voyage alone; you consented to take me; I will sacrifice myself! I shall drop into the water, and the balloon, relieved of my weight, will mount again.'

" ' No, no! It is frightful!'

" The balloon became less and less inflated, and as it doubled up its concavity pressed the gas against the sides and hastened its downward course.

" ' Adieu,' said the doctor ' God preserve you!'

" He was about to throw himself over, when Blanchard held him back.

" ' There is one more chance.' said he. ' We can cut the

cords which hold the car, and cling to the net! Perhaps the balloon will rise. Let us hold ourselves ready. But— the barometer is going down! The wind is freshening! We are saved!'

"The aeronauts perceived Calais. Their joy was delirious. A few moments more, and they had fallen in the forest of Guines. I do not doubt," added the unknown, "that, under similar circumstances, you would have followed Doctor Jeffries' example!"

The clouds rolled in glittering masses beneath us. The balloon threw large shadows on them, and was surrounded as by an aureola. The thunder rumbled below the car. All this was terrifying. "Let us descend!" I cried.

"Descend, when the sun is up there, waiting for us? Out with more bags!"

And more than fifty pounds of ballast were cast over.

At a height of three thousand five hundred yards we remained stationary. The unknown talked unceasingly. I was in a state of complete prostration, while he seemed to be in his element. "With a good wind, we shall go far," he cried. "In the Antilles there are currents of air which have a speed of a hundred leagues an hour. When Napoleon was crowned, Garnerin sent up a balloon with colored lamps, at eleven o'clock at night. The wind was blowing north-north-west. The next morning, at daybreak, the inhabitants of Rome greeted its passage over the dome of St Peter's. We shall go farther and higher!"

I scarcely heard him. Everything whirled around me. An opening appeared in the clouds.

"See that city," said the unknown. "It is Spires!"

I leaned over the car and perceived a small blackish mass. It was Spires. The Rhine, which is so large, seemed an unrolled ribbon. The sky was a deep blue over our heads. The birds had long abandoned us, for in that rarefied air they could not have flown. We were alone in space, and I in the presence of this unknown!

"It is useless for you to know whither I am leading you," he said, as he threw the compass among the clouds. "Ah! a fall is a grand thing! You know that but few victims of ballooning are to be reckoned, from Pilâtre des Rosiers to Lieutenant Gale, and that the accidents have always been the result of imprudence. Pilâtre des Rosiers set out with

Romain of Boulogne, on the 13th of June, 1785. To his gas balloon he had affixed a Montgolfier apparatus of hot air, so as to dispense, no doubt, with the necessity of losing gas or throwing out ballast. It was putting a torch under a powder-barrel. When they had ascended four hundred yards, and were taken by opposing winds, they were driven over the open sea. Pilâtre, in order to descend, essayed to open the valve, but the valve-cord became entangled in the balloon, and tore it so badly that it became empty in an instant. It fell upon the Montgolfier apparatus, overturned it, and dragged down the unfortunates, who were soon shattered to pieces! It is frightful, is it not?"

I could only reply, " For pity's sake let us descend!"

The clouds gathered around us on every side, and dreadful detonations, which reverberated in the cavity of the balloon, took place beneath us.

"You provoke me," cried the unknown, " and you shall no longer know whether we are rising or falling!"

The barometer went the way of the compass, accompanied by several more bags of sand. We must have been 5000 yards high. Some icicles had already attached themselves to the sides of the car, and a kind of fine snow seemed to penetrate to my very bones. Meanwhile a frightful tempest was raging under us, but we were above it.

"Do not be afraid," said the unknown. "It is only the imprudent who are lost. Olivari, who perished at Orleans, rose in a paper 'Montgolfier;' his car, suspended below the chafing-dish, and ballasted with combustible materials, caught fire; Olivari fell, and was killed! Mosment rose, at Lille, on a light tray; an oscillation disturbed his equilibrium; Mosment fell, and was killed! Bittorf, at Manuheim, saw his balloon catch fire in the air; and he, too, fell, and was killed! Harris rose in a badly constructed balloon, the valve of which was too large and would not shut; Harris fell, and was killed! Sadler, deprived of ballast by his long sojourn in the air, was dragged over the town of Boston and dashed against the chimneys; Sadler fell, and was killed! Cokling descended with a convex parachute which he pretended to have perfected; Cokling fell, and was killed! Well, I love them, these victims of their own imprudence, and I shall die as they did. Higher! still higher!"

All the phantoms of this necrology passed before my

eyes. The rarefaction of the air and the sun's rays added to the expansion of the gas, and the balloon continued to mount. I tried to open the valve, but the unknown cut the cord several feet above my head. I was lost.

"Did you see Madame Blanchard fall?" said he. "I saw her; yes, I! I was at Tivoli on the 6th of July, 1819. Madame Blanchard rose in a small-sized balloon, to avoid the expense of filling, and she was forced to inflate it entirely. The gas leaked out below, and left a regular train of hydrogen in its path. She carried with her a sort of pyrotechnic aureola, suspended below her car by a wire, which she was to set off in the air. This she had done many times before. On this day she also carried up a small parachute ballasted by a firework contrivance, that would go off in a shower of silver. She was to start this contrivance after having lighted it with a port-fire made on purpose. She set out; the night was gloomy. At the moment of lighting her fireworks she was so imprudent as to pass the taper under the column of hydrogen which was leaking from the balloon. My eyes were fixed upon her. Suddenly an unexpected gleam lit up the darkness. I thought she was preparing a surprise. The light flashed out, suddenly disappeared and reappeared, and gave the summit of the balloon the shape of an immense jet of ignited gas. This sinister glow shed itself over the Boulevard and the whole Montmarrte quarter. Then I saw the unhappy woman rise, try twice to close the appendage of the balloon, so as to put out the fire, then sit down in her car and try to guide her descent; for she did not fall. The combustion of the gas lasted for several minutes. The balloon, becoming gradually less, continued to descend, but it was not a fall. The wind blew from the north-west and drove it towards Paris. There were then some large gardens just by the house No. 16, Rue de Provence. Madame Blanchard essayed to fall there without danger; but the ballon and the car struck on the roof of the house with a light shock. 'Save me!' cried the wretched woman. I got into the street at this moment. The car slid along the roof, and encountered an iron cramp. Madame Blanchard was thrown out of her car and precipitated upon the pavement She was killed!"

These stories froze me with horror. The unknown was

standing with bare head, disheveled hair, haggard eyes! There was no longer any illusion possible. I recognized the horrible truth. I was in the presence of a madman!

He threw out the rest of the ballast, and we must have now reached a height of at least nine thousand yards. Blood spurted from my nose and mouth!

"Who are nobler than the martyrs of science?" cried the lunatic. "They are canonized by posterity."

But I no longer heard him. He bent down to my ear and muttered, "And have you forgotten Zambecarri's catastrophe? Listen. On the 7th of October, 1804, the clouds seemed to lift a little. On the preceding days, the wind and rain had not ceased; but the announced ascension of Zambecarri could not be postponed. His enemies were already bantering him. It was necessary to ascend to save the science and himself from becoming a public jest. It was at Boulogne. No one helped him to inflate his balloon. He rose at midnight, accompanied by Andreoli and Grossetti. The balloon mounted slowly, for it had been perforated by the rain, and the gas was leaking out. The three intrepid aeronauts could only observe the state of the barometer by aid of a dark lantern. Zambecarri had eaten nothing for twenty-four hours. Grossetti was also fasting.

"'My friends,' said Zambecarri, 'I am overcome by cold, and exhausted. I am dying.'

"He fell inanimate in the gallery. It was the same with Grossetti. Andreoli alone remained conscious. After long efforts, he succeeded in reviving Zambecarri.

"'What news? Whither are we going? How is the wind? What time is it?'

"'It is two o'clock.'

"'Where is the compass?'

"'Upset!'

"'Great God! The lantern has gone out!'

"'It cannot burn in this rarefied air," said Zambecarri.

"The moon had not risen and the atmosphere was plunged in murky darkness. "'I am cold, Andreoli. What shall I do?'

"They slowly descended through a layer of whitish clouds. 'Sh!' said Andreoli. 'Do you hear?'

"'What?' asked Zambecarri.

" ' A strange noise.'

" ' You are mistaken. Consider these travelers, in the middle of the night, listening to that unaccountable noise! Are they going to knock against a tower? Are they about to be precipitated on the roofs? ' Do you hear? One would say it was the sea.'

" ' Impossible! '

" ' It is the groaning of the waves! '

" ' It is true.'

" ' Light! light! ' After five fruitless attempts, Andreoli succeeded in obtaining light. It was three o'clock.

" The voice of violent waves was heard. They were almost touching the surface of the sea! ' We are lost! ' cried Zambecarri, seizing a bag of sand.

" ' Help! ' cried Andreoli.

" The car touched the water, and the waves came up to their breasts. ' Throw out the instruments, clothes! '

" The aeronauts completely stripped themselves. The balloon, relieved, rose with frightful rapidity. Zambecarri was taken with vomiting. Grossetti bled profusely. The unfortunate men could not speak, so short was their breathing. They were taken with cold, and they were soon crusted over with ice. The moon looked as red as blood.

" After traversing the high regions for a half-hour, the balloon again fell into the sea. It was four in the morning. They were half submerged in the water, and the balloon dragged them along, as if under sail, for several hours.

" At daybreak they found themselves opposite Pesaro, four miles from the coast. They were about to reach it, when a gale blew them back into the open sea. They were lost! The frightened boats fled at their approach Happily, a more intelligent boatman accosted them, hoisted them on board, and they landed at Ferrada.

" A frightful journey, was it not? But Zambecarri was a brave and energetic man. Scarcely recovered from his sufferings, he resumed his ascensions. During one of them he struck against a tree; his spirit-lamp was broken on his clothes; he was enveloped in fire, his balloon began to catch the flames, and he came down half consumed.

" At last, on the 21st of September, 1812, he made another ascension at Boulogne. The balloon clung to a tree, and his lamp again set it on fire. Zambecarri fell, and was killed! And in presence of these facts, we would still hesitate! No. The higher we go, the more glorious will be our death!"

The balloon being now entirely relieved of ballast and of all it contained, we were carried to an enormous height. It vibrated in the atmosphere. The least noise resounded in the vaults of heaven. Our globe, the only object which caught my view in immensity, seemed ready to be annihilated, and above us the depths of the starry skies were lost in thick darkness.

I saw my companion rise up before me.

"The hour is come!" he said. "We must die. We are rejected of men. They despise us. We will not endure it. Let us crush them!"

"Mercy!" I cried.

"Let us cut these cords! Let this car be abandoned in space. The attractive force will change its direction, and we shall approach the sun!"

Despair galvanized me. I threw myself upon the madman, we struggled together, and a terrible conflict took place. But I was thrown down, and while he held me under his knee, the madman was cutting the cords of the car "One!" he cried.

"My God!"

"Two! Three!"

I made a superhuman effort, rose up, and violently repulsed the madman.

"Four!" The car fell, but I instinctively clung to the cords and hoisted myself into the meshes of the netting.

The madman disappeared in space!

The balloon rose to an immeasurable height. A horrible cracking was heard. The gas, too much dilated, had burst the balloon. I shut my eyes——

Some instants after, a damp warmth revived me. I was in the midst of clouds on fire. The balloon turned over with dizzy velocity. Taken by the wind, it made a hundred leagues an hour in a horizontal course, the lightning flashing around it.

Meanwhile my fall was not a very rapid one. When I opened my eyes, I saw the country. I was two miles from the sea, and the tempest was driving me violently towards it, when an abrupt shock forced me to loosen my hold. My hands opened, a cord slipped swiftly between my fingers, and I found myself on the solid earth!

It was the cord of the anchor, which, sweeping along the surface of the ground, was caught in a crevice; and my balloon, unballasted for the last time, careered off to lose itself beyond the sea.

When I came to myself, I was in bed in a peasant's cottage, at Harderwick, a village of La Gueldre, fifteen leagues from Amsterdam, on the shores of the Zuyder-Zee.

A miracle had saved my life, but my voyage had been a series of imprudences, committed by a lunatic, and I had not been able to prevent them.

May this terrible narrative, though instructing those who read it, not discourage the explorers of the air.

THE END

The Watch's Soul

OR

Master Zacharius

The Watch's Soul

CHAPTER I
A WINTER'S NIGHT

THE city of Geneva is situated at the western extremity of the lake to which it gives—or owes —its name. The Rhone, which crosses the city on emerging from the lake, divides it into two distinct quarters, and is itself divided, in the center of the city, by an island rising between its two banks. This topographical situation is often to be observed in the great centers of commerce or industry. Doubtless the earliest inhabitants were seduced by the facilities of transportation afforded by the rapid arms of the rivers,—"those roads which advance of themselves," as Pascal says. In the case of the Rhone, they are roads which run. At the period when new and regular buildings had not as yet been erected on this island, anchored like a Dutch galiot in the midst of the river, the wonderful mass of houses huddled the one against the other offered to the eye a confusion full of charms. The small extent of the island had forced some of these buildings to perch upon piles, fastened pell-mell in the strong currents of the Rhone. These big timbers, blackened by time and worn by the waters, looked like the claws of an immense crab, and produced a fantastic effect. Some yellowed nets, real spiders' webs stretched amid these venerable substructures, shivered and trembled in the shade as if they had been the foliage of these old oaks, and the river, engulfing itself in the midst of this forest of piles, foamed with melancholy groans.

One of the habitations on the island struck the observer by its strange appearance of extreme age. It was the residence of the old clockmaker, Master Zacharius, his daughter Gerande, Aubert Thun, his apprentice, and his old servant, Scholastique.

What an original personage was this Zacharius! His age seemed incalculable. The oldest inhabitants of Geneva could not have told how long his lean head had wavered on his shoulders, nor the first day on which he had been seen walking along the streets of the town, his long white locks floating waywardly in the wind. This man did not live. He oscillated after the manner of the pendulums of his clocks. His features, dry and cadaverous, affected somber tints. Like the pictures of Leonardo da Vinci, he had put black in the foreground.

Gerande occupied the best room in the old house; whence, through a narrow window, her gaze rested sadly upon the snowy summits of the Jura. But the bedroom and shop of the old man were in a sort of cellar, situated on a level with the river; the flooring rested on the piles themselves. From an immemorial period Master Zacharius had not been known to emerge thence, except at meal-time, and when he went forth to regulate the different clocks of the city. He passed the rest of the time at a bench covered with numerous clockmaking instruments, which, for the most part, he had himself invented.

For he was a man of talent. His works were very popular throughout France and Germany. The most industrious workmen in Geneva freely admitted his superiority, and that he was an honor to the city. They pointed him out, saying, "To him is due the glory of having invented the escapement!"

Indeed, it is from this invention, which the labors of Zacharius will later make clear, that is to be dated the birth of the real science of clockmaking.

One winter's evening old Scholastique was serving supper, in which, according to ancient usage, she was aided by the young apprentice. Though carefully prepared dishes were offered to Master Zacharius in fine blue-and-white porcelain, he ate nothing. He scarcely replied to the soft questionings of Gerande, who was visibly affected by the gloomy silence of her father; and the garrulousness of Scholastique herself only struck his ear like the grumblings of the river, to which he no longer paid attention. After this silent repast the old clockmaker left the table without embracing his daughter, nor did he, as usual, bid the rest " good-evening." He disappeared through the narrow door which conducted to his retreat, and the staircase fairly creaked under his heavy tread.

Gerande, Aubert, and Scholastique remained silent for some moments. The weather was gloomy; the clouds

dragged themselves heavily along the Alps, and threatened
to dissolve in rain; the severe temperature of Switzerland
filled the soul with melancholy, while the midland winds
prowled among the hills and whistled drearily.

"Do you know, my dear demoiselle," said Scholastique
at last, "that our master has kept wholly to himself for
some days? Holy Virgin! I see he has not been hungry,
for his words have remained in his stomach, and the Devil
himself would be adroit to force one out of him!"

"My father has some secret trouble which I cannot even
guess," replied Gerande, a sad anxiety betraying itself in
her countenance.

"Mademoiselle, do not permit so much sadness to over-
shadow your heart. You know the singular habits of Master Zacharius. Who can read his secret thoughts in his
face? Something annoying has no doubt happened to him,
but he will have forgotten it by to-morrow, and will repent
having made his daughter anxious."

It was Aubert who spoke thus, glancing at Gerande's
lovely eyes. Aubert was the first apprentice whom Master
Zacharius had ever admitted to the intimacy of his labors,
for he appreciated his intelligence, discretion, and goodness
of heart; and this young man had attached himself to
Gerande with that mysterious faith which presides over
heroic denouements.

Gerande was eighteen years of age. The oval of her
face recalled that of the artless Madonnas, whom venera-
tion still displays at the street corners of the antique towns
of Brittany. Her eyes betrayed an infinite simplicity.
She was beloved as the most delicate realization of a poet's
dream. Whilst, night and morning, she read her Latin
prayers in her iron-clasped missal, Gerande also discovered
a hidden sentiment in Aubert Thun's heart, and comprehended what a profound devotion the young workman had
for her. Indeed, the whole world in his eyes was con-
densed in this old house of the clockmaker, and he passed
all his time near the young girl, when, the hours of work
over, he left her father's workshop.

Old Scholastique saw all this, but said nothing. Her
loquacity exhausted itself in preference on the evils of the
times, and the little worries of the household. Nobody
tried to stop its course. It was with her as with the musi-

cal snuff-boxes which they made at Geneva; once wound up, unless you broke her, she would play all her airs through.

Finding Gerande absorbed in a melancholy silence, Scholastique left her old wooden chair, fixed a taper on the end of a candlestick, lit it, and placed it near a small waxen Virgin, sheltered in her niche of stone. It was the family custom to kneel before this protecting Madonna of the domestic hearth, and to beg her kindly watchfulness during the coming night; but on this evening, Gerande remained silent in her seat.

" Well, well, dear demoiselle," said the astonished Scholastique, " supper is over, and it is time to go to bed. Why do you tire your eyes by sitting up late? Ah, Holy Virgin! It is much better to sleep, and to get a little comfort from happy dreams! In these detestable times in which we live, who can promise herself a fortunate day? "

" Ought we not to send for a doctor for my father? " asked Gerande.

" A doctor! " cried the old domestic. " Has Master Zacharius ever listened to their fancies and pompous sayings? He might accept medicines for the watches, but not for the body! "

" What shall we do? " murmured Gerande. " Has he gone to work, or has he retired? "

" Gerande," answered Aubert, softly, " some mental trouble annoys your father, and that is all."

" Do you know what it is, Aubert? "

" Perhaps, Gerande."

" Tell us, then," cried Scholastique, eagerly, prudently extinguishing her taper.

" For several days, Gerande," said the young apprentice, " something absolutely incomprehensible has been going on. All the watches which your father has made and sold for some years have suddenly stopped. Very many of them have been brought back to him. He has carefully taken them to pieces; the springs were in good condition, and the wheels well set. He has put them together yet more carefully; but, despite his skill, they have refused to go."

" The devil's in it! " cried Scholastique.

" Why say you so? " asked Gerande. " It seems very

natural to me. All things are limited in the world. The infinite cannot be fashioned by the hands of men."

"It is none the less true," returned Aubert, "that there is in this something very mysterious and extraordinary. I have myself been helping Master Zacharius to search for the cause of this derangement of his watches; but I have not been able to find it, and more than once I have despairingly let my tools fall from my hands."

"But why undertake so vain a task?" resumed Scholastique. "Is it natural that a little copper instrument should go of itself, and mark the hours? We ought to have kept to the sun-dial!"

"You will not talk thus, Scholastique," said Aubert, "when you learn that the sun-dial was invented by Cain."

"O Lord! what are you telling me?"

"Do you think," asked Gerande, simply, "that we might pray to God to give life to my father's watches?"

"Without doubt," replied Aubert.

"Good! These will be useless prayers," grumbled the old servant, "but Heaven will pardon them for their good intent."

The taper was relighted. Scholastique, Gerande, and Aubert knelt down together upon the flags of the room. The young girl prayed for her mother's soul, for a blessing for the night, for travelers and prisoners, for the good and the wicked, and more earnestly than all for the unknown misfortunes of her father. Then the three devout souls rose with somewhat of confidence in their hearts, for they had laid their sorrow in God's bosom.

Aubert repaired to his own room; Gerande sat pensively by the window, whilst the last lights were disappearing from the city streets. The terrors of this winter's night had increased. Sometimes, with the whirlpools of the river, the wind engulfed itself among the piles, and the whole house shivered and shook; but the young girl, absorbed in her sadness, thought only of her father. After hearing what Aubert told her, the malady of Master Zacharius took fantastic proportions in her mind; and it seemed to her as if his dear existence, become purely mechanical, moved now with pain and effort on its exhausted pivots.

Suddenly the shutters, impelled by the squall, struck against the windows of the room. The young girl leaned out of the window to draw to the shutter shaken by the wind, but she feared to do so. It seemed to her that the rain and the river, confounding their tumultous waters, were submerging the frail house, the planks of which were creaking in every direction. She would have flown from her chamber, but she saw below the flickering of a light which appeared to come from Master Zacharius's retreat, and in one of those momentary calms, during which the elements keep a sudden silence, her ear caught plaintive sounds. She tried to shut her window, but could not. The wind violently repelled her, like a villain who was introducing himself into a dwelling.

Gerande thought she would go mad from terror. What was her father doing? She opened the door, and it escaped from her hands, and shook loudly under the attack of the tempest. Gerande then found herself in the dark supper-room, succeeded in gaining, on tiptoe, the staircase which led to her father's shop, and, pale and fainting, glided down.

The old watchmaker was upright in the middle of the room, which was filled with the groans of the river. His bristling hair gave him a sinister aspect. He was talking and gesticulating, without seeing or hearing anything. Gerande arrested her steps on the threshold.

"It is death!" said Master Zacharius, in a thick voice; "it is death! Why should I live longer, now that I have dispersed my existence over the earth? For I, Master Zacharius, am really the creator of all the watches that I have fashioned! It is a part of my very soul that I have shut up in each of these boxes of iron, silver, or gold! Every time that one of these accursed watches stops, I feel my heart cease beating, for I have regulated them with its pulsations!"

As he spoke in this strange way, the old man cast his eyes on his bench. There lay all the pieces of a watch that he had carefully taken apart. He took up a sort of hollow cylinder, called a barrel, in which the spring is enclosed, and removed the steel spiral, which, instead of relaxing itself, according to the laws of its elasticity, remained coiled on itself, like a sleeping viper. It seemed knotted like those impotent old men whose blood has long been congealed. Master Zacharius vainly essayed to uncoil it with his thin fingers, the outlines of which were exaggerated on the wall; but he tried in vain, and soon, with a terrible cry of anguish and rage, he threw it through the peephole into the boiling Rhone.

Gerande, her feet riveted to the floor, stood breathless and motionless. She wished to approach her father, but could not. Giddy hallucinations took possession of her. Suddenly she heard, in the shade, a voice murmur in her ears, "Gerande, dear Gerande! grief still keeps you awake! Go in again, I beg of you; the night is cold."

"Aubert!" whispered the young girl. "You!"

"Ought I not to be disturbed by what disturbs you?"

These soft words sent the blood back into the young girl's heart. She leaned on Aubert's arm, and said to him, "My father is very ill, Aubert! You alone can cure him, for this disorder of the mind would not yield to his daughter's consolings. His mind is attacked by a very natural delusion, and in working with him, repairing the watches, you will bring him back to reason. Aubert," she continued, "it is not true, is it, that his life confounds itself with that of his watches?"

Aubert did not reply.

"Then it must be a calling reproved of God—that of my father?"

"I know not," returned the apprentice, warming the cold hands of the girl with his own. "But go back to your room, my poor Gerande, and with sleep recover hope!"

Gerande slowly returned to her chamber, and remained there till daylight; sleep did not weigh down her eyelids. Meanwhile, Master Zacharius, always mute and motionless, gazed at the river as it rolled turbulently at his feet.

CHAPTER II
THE PRIDE OF SCIENCE

THE severity of a Geneva merchant in business matters has become proverbial. He is rigidly honorable, and excessively just. What must, then, have been the shame of Master Zacharius, when he saw these watches, which he had so carefully constructed, returning to him from every direction?

It was certain that these watches had suddenly stopped, and without any apparent reason. The wheels were in a good condition and firmly fixed, but the springs had lost all elasticity. Vainly did the watchmaker try to replace them; the wheels remained motionless. These unaccountable derangements were greatly to the old man's discredit. His noble inventions had many times brought upon him suspicions of sorcery, which now seemed confirmed. These rumors reached Gerande, and she often trembled for her father, when she saw the malicious glances directed towards him.

Yet on the morning after this night of anguish, Master Zacharius seemed to resume work with some confidence. The morning sun inspired him with some courage. Aubert hastened to join him in the shop, and received an affable "good-day."

"I am getting on better," said the old man. "I don't know what strange troubles of the head attacked me yesterday, but the sun has quite chased them away, with the clouds of the night."

"In faith, master," returned Aubert, "I don't like the night for either of us!"

"And thou art right, Aubert. If you ever become a superior man, you will understand that day is as necessary to you as food. A man of merit owes himself to the homage of the rest of mankind who recognize his worth."

"Master, it seems to me that the pride of science has possessed you."

"Pride, Aubert! Destroy my past, annihilate my present, dissipate my future, and then it will be permitted to me to live in obscurity! Poor boy, who comprehends not the sublime things to which my art is wholly devoted! Art thou not but a tool in my hands?"

"Yet, Master Zacharius," resumed Aubert, "I have more than once merited your praise for the manner in which I adjusted the most delicate pieces of your watches and clocks."

"No doubt, Aubert; thou art a good workman, such as I love; but when thou workest, thou thinkest thou hast in thy hands but copper, silver, gold; thou dost not perceive these metals, which my genius animates, palpitating like living flesh! Thus thou wouldst not die, with the death of thy works!"

Master Zacharius remained silent after these words; but Aubert essayed to keep up the conversation. "Indeed, master," said he, "I love to see you work so unceasingly! You will be ready for the festival of our corporation, for I see that the work on this crystal watch is going forward famously."

"No doubt, Aubert," cried the old watchmaker, "and it will be no slight honor for me to have been able to cut and shape the crystal to the durability of a diamond! Ah, Louis Berghen did well to perfect the art of diamond-cutting, which has enabled me to polish and pierce the hardest stones!"

Master Zacharius was holding several small watch pieces of cut crystal, and of exquisite workmanship. The wheels, pivots, and box of the watch were of the same material, and he had employed remarkable skill in this very difficult task. "Would it not be fine," said he, his face flushing, "to see this watch palpitating beneath its transparent envelope, and to be able to count the very beatings of its heart?"

"I will wager, sir," replied the young apprentice, "that it will not vary a second in a year."

"And you would wager on a certainty! Have I not imparted to it all that is purest of myself? And does my heart itself vary?"

Aubert did not dare to lift his eyes to his master's transfigured face.

"Tell me frankly," said the old man, sadly. "Have you never taken me for a fool? Do you not think me sometimes subject to dangerous folly? Yes; is it not? In my daughter's eyes and yours, I have often read my condemnation. Oh!" he cried, as if in pain, "to be not understood by those whom one most loves in the world! But I will prove victoriously to thee, Aubert, that I am right! Do not bow thy head, for thou wilt be stupefied. The day on which thou understandest how to listen to and comprehend me, thou wilt see that I have discovered the secrets of existence, the secrets of the mysterious union of the soul with the body!"

As he spoke thus, Master Zacharius appeared superb in

his vanity. His eyes glittered with a supernatural fire, and his pride illumined every feature. And truly, if ever vanity was excusable, it was such vanity as that of Master Zacharius!

The watchmaker's art, indeed, down to his time, had remained almost in its infancy. From the day when Plato, four centuries before the Christian era, invented the night watch, a sort of clepsydra which indicated the hours of the night by the sound and playing of a flute, the science had continued nearly stationary. The masters paid more attention to the arts than to mechanics, and it was the period of beautiful watches of iron, copper, wood, silver, which were richly engraved. like one of Cellini's ewers. They made a masterpiece of chasing, which measured time very imperfectly, but was still a masterpiece. When the artist's imagination was not directed to the perfection of modeling, it sought to create clocks with moving figures and melodious sounds, which were put in operation in a very diverting fashion. Besides, who troubled himself, in those days, with regulating the advance of the hours? The delays of the law were not as yet invented; the physical and astronomical sciences had not as yet established their calculations on scrupulously exact measurements; there were neither establishments which were shut at a given hour, nor trains which departed at a precise moment. In the evening the curfew bell sounded; and at night the hours were cried amid the universal silence. Certainly people did not live so long, if existence is measured by the amount of business done; but they lived better. The mind was enriched with the noble sentiments born of the contemplation of masterpieces. They built a church in two centuries, a painter painted but few pictures in the course of his life, a poet only composed one great work; but these were so many masterpieces.

When the exact sciences began at last to make some progress, watch and clock making followed in their path, though it was always arrested by an insurmountable difficulty,— the regular and continuous measurement of time.

It was in the midst of this stagnation that Master Zacharius invented the escapement, which enabled him to obtain a mathematical regularity by submitting the movement of the pendulum to a constant force. This invention had turned the old man's head. Pride, swelling in his heart, like mercury in the thermometer, had attained the height of transcendent folly. By analogy he had allowed himself to be drawn to materialistic conclusions, and as he constructed his watches, he fancied that he had surprised the hitherto undiscovered secrets of the union of the soul with the body.

So it was that, on this day, perceiving that Aubert listened to him attentively, he said to him in a tone of simple conviction, "Dost thou know what life is, my child? Hast thou comprehended the action of those springs which produce existence? Hast thou examined thyself? No; and yet, with the eyes of science, thou mightst have seen the intimate relation which exists between God's work and my own, for it is from his creature that I have copied the combinations of the wheels of my clocks."

"Master," replied Aubert, eagerly, "can you compare a copper or steel machine with that breath of God which is called the soul, which animates our bodies, as the breeze lends motion to the flowers? What mechanism could be so adjusted as to inspire us with thought?"

"That is not the question," responded Master Zacharius, gently, but with all the obstinacy of a blind man walking towards an abyss. "In order to understand me, thou must recall the object of the escapement which I have invented. When I saw the irregular working of clocks, I understood that the movements shut up in them did not suffice, and that it was necessary to submit them to the regularity of some independent force. I then thought that the balance-wheel might accomplish this, and I succeeded in regulating the movement! Now, was it not a sublime idea that came to me, to return to it its lost force by the action of the clock itself, which it was charged with regulating?"

Aubert assented by a motion.

"Now, Aubert," continued the old man, growing animated, "cast thine eyes upon thyself! Dost thou not understand that there are two distinct forces in us, that of the soul and that of the body, that is, a movement and a regulator? The soul is the principle of life; that is, then, the movement. Whether it is produced by a weight, by a spring, or by an immaterial influence, it is none the less

at the heart. But without the body this movement would
be unequal, irregular, impossible! Thus the body regu-
lates the soul, and, like the balance-wheel, it is submitted to
regular oscillations. And this is so true, that one falls ill
when one's drink, food, sleep—in a word, the functions of
the body—are not properly regulated! As in my watches,
the soul renders to the body the force lost by its oscillations. Well, what produces this intimate union between
soul and body, if not a marvelous escapement, by which
the wheels of the one work into the wheels of the other?
This is what I have divined, applied; and there are no
longer any secrets for me in this life, which is, after all,
but an ingenious mechanism!"

Master Zacharius was sublime to see in this hallucina-
tion, which transported him to the ultimate mysteries of
the infinite. But his daughter Gerande, standing on the
threshold of the door, had heard all. She rushed into her
father's arms, and he pressed her convulsively to his breast.

"What is the matter with thee, my daughter?" he
asked.

"If I had only a spring here," said she, putting her
hand on her heart, "I would not love you as I do, my
father."

Master Zacharius looked intently at Gerande, and did
not reply. Suddenly he uttered a cry, carried his hand
eagerly to his heart, and fell fainting on his old leathern
chair.

"Father, what is the matter?"

"Help!" cried Aubert. "Scholastique!"

But Scholastique did not come at once. Someone was
knocking at the front door; she had gone to open it, and
when she returned to the shop, before she could open her
mouth, the old watchmaker, having recovered his senses,
spoke: "I divine, my old Scholastique, that you bring me
still another of those accursed watches which have
stopped."

"O Lord, it is true enough!" replied Scholastique, hand-
ing a watch to Aubert.

"My heart could not be mistaken!" said the old man,
with a sigh.

Aubert carefully adjusted the watch, but it would not go.

CHAPTER III
A STRANGE VISIT

POOR Gerande would have lost her life with that of her father, had it not been for the thought of Aubert, who still attached her to the world. The old watchmaker was, little by little, passing away. His faculties evidently grew more feeble, as he concentrated them on a single thought. By a sad association of ideas, he referred everything to his monomania, and human existence seemed to have departed from him. Moreover, certain malicious rivals revived the hostile rumors which had spread concerning his labors.

The news of the strange derangements which his watches betrayed had a prodigious effect upon the master clockmakers of Geneva. What signified this sudden inertia of their wheels, and why these strange relations which they seemed to have with the old man's life? These were the kind of mysteries which people never contemplate without a secret terror. In the various classes of the town, from the apprentices to the great lords who used his watches, there was no one who could not himself judge of the singularity of the fact. The citizens wished, but in vain, to penetrate to Master Zacharius. He fell very ill; and this enabled his daughter to withdraw him from incessant visits, which thereupon degenerated into reproaches and recriminations.

Medicines and physicians were powerless in presence of this organic wasting away, the cause of which could not be discovered. It sometimes seemed as if the old man's heart had ceased to beat; then the pulsations were resumed with an alarming irregularity.

A custom existed, in those days, of submitting the works of the masters to the judgment of the people. The heads of the various corporations sought to distinguish themselves by the novelty or the perfection of their productions, and it was among these that the condition of Master Zacharius excited the most lively, because most interested, commiseration. His rivals pitied him the more willingly, the less he was to be feared. They never forgot the old man's success, when he exhibited his magnificent clocks with moving figures, his striking watches, which provoked the general admiration, and commanded such high prices in the cities of France, Switzerland, and Germany.

Meanwhile, thanks to the constant and tender care of

Gerande and Aubert, his strength seemed to return a little,
and in the tranquillity in which his convalescence left him,
he succeeded in detaching himself from the thoughts which
had absorbed him. As soon as he could walk, his daughter
lured him away from the house, which was still besieged
with dissatisfied intruders. Aubert remained in the shop,
vainly adjusting and readjusting the rebel watches; and the
poor boy, completely mystified, sometimes covered his face
in his hands, fearful that he, like his master, might go mad.

So it came about that the old watchmaker at last perceived that he was not alone in the world. As he looked
upon his young and lovely daughter, himself old and
broken, he reflected that after his death she would be left
alone, without support. Many of the young mechanics of
Geneva had already sought to win Gerande's love; but none
of them had succeeded in gaining access to the impenetrable
retreat of the watchmaker's household. It was natural,
then, that during this lucid interval the old man's choice
should fall on Aubert Thun. Once struck with this
thought, he remarked to himself that this young couple
had been brought up with the same ideas and the same be-
liefs, and the oscillations of their hearts seemed to him, as
he said one day to Scholastique, " isochronal."

The old servant, literally delighted with the word, though
she did not understand it, swore by her holy patron saint
that the whole town should hear it within a quarter of an
hour. Master Zacharius found it difficult to calm her, but
made her promise to keep on this subject a silence which
she never was known to observe.

So, though Gerande and Aubert were ignorant of it,
all Geneva was soon talking of their speedy union. But
it happened also that, while the worthy folk were gossiping,
a strange chuckle was often heard, and a voice saying,
" Gerande will not wed Aubert."

If the gossipers turned round, they found themselves
facing a little old man who was quite a stranger to them.

How old was this singular being? No one could have
told. People conjectured that he must have existed for
several centuries, and that was all. His big flat head rested
upon shoulders the width of which was equal to the height
of his body; this was not above three feet. This personage would have figured well on a pendulum fulcrum, for

the dial would have naturally been placed on his face, and the balance-wheel would have oscillated at its ease in his chest. His nose might readily be taken for the style of a sun-dial, for it was small and sharp; his teeth, far apart, resembled the gearing of a wheel, and ground themselves between his lips; his voice had the metallic sound of a bell, and you could hear his heart beat like the tick-tick of a clock. This little man, whose arms moved like the needles on a dial, walked with jerks, without ever turning round. If anyone followed him, it was found that he walked a league an hour, and that his course was nearly circular.

This strange being had not long been seen wandering, or rather circulating, around the town; but it had already been observed that, every day, at the moment when the sun passed the meridian, he stopped before the Cathedral of Saint Pierre, and resumed his course after the twelve strokes of midday had sounded. Excepting at this precise moment, he seemed to become a part of all the conversations in which the old watchmaker was talked of, and people asked each other, in terror, what relation could exist between him and Master Zacharius. It was remarked, too, that he never lost sight of the old man and his daughter while they were taking their promenades.

One day Gerande perceived this monster looking at her with a hideous smile. She clung to her father with a frightened motion.

"What is the matter, my Gerande?" asked Master Zacharius.

"I do not know," replied the young girl.

"But thou art changed, my child. Art thou going to fall ill in thy turn? Ah, well," he added, with a sad smile, "then I must take care of thee, and I will do it tenderly."

"O father, it will be nothing. I am cold, and I imagine that it is——"

"What, Gerande?"

"The presence of that man, who always follows us," she replied in a low tone.

Master Zacharius turned towards the little old man. "Faith, he goes well," said he, with a satisfied air, "for it is just four o'clock. Fear nothing, my child; it is not a man, it is a clock!"

Gerande looked at her father in terror. How could

Master Zacharius read the hour on this strange creature's visage?

"By the by," continued the old watchmaker, paying no further attention to the matter, "I have not seen Aubert for several days."

"He has not left us, however, father," said Gerande, whose thoughts turned into a gentler channel.

"What is he doing, then?"

"He is working."

"Ah!" cried the old man. "He is at work repairing my watches, is he not? But he will never succeed; for it is not repairs they need, but a resurrection!"

Gerande remained silent.

"I must know," added the old man, "if they have brought back any more of those damned watches, upon which the Devil has imposed an epidemic!"

After these words Master Zacharius fell into absolute taciturnity, till he knocked at the door of his house, and for the first time since his convalescence descended to his shop, while Gerande sadly repaired to her chamber.

At this moment when Master Zacharius crossed the threshold of his shop, one of the many clocks suspended on the wall struck five o'clock. Usually the bells of these clocks—admirably regulated as they were—struck simultaneously, and this rejoiced the old man's heart; but on this day the bells struck one after another, so that for a quarter of an hour the ear was deafened by the successive noise. Master Zacharius suffered terribly; he could not remain still, but went from one clock to the other, and beat the measure for them, as an orchestra leader who has no longer control over his musicians.

When the last had ceased striking, the door of the shop opened, and Master Zacharius shuddered from head to foot to see before him the little old man, who looked fixedly at him and said, "Master, may I not speak with you a few moments?"

"Who are you?" asked the watchmaker, abruptly.

"A colleague. I am charged with regulating the sun."

"Ah, you regulate the sun!" replied Master Zacharius, eagerly, without wincing. "I can scarcely compliment you upon it. Your sun goes badly, to make ourselves agree with it, we have to keep advancing and retarding our clocks!"

"And, by the Devil's cloven foot," cried this weird personage, "you are right, my master! My sun does not always indicate midday at the same moment as your clocks; but some day it will be known that this is because of the inequality of the movement of the earth's transfer, and a mean midday will be invented which will regulate this irregularity!"

"Shall I live till then?" asked the old man, with glistening eyes.

"Without doubt," replied the little old man, laughing. "Can you believe that you will ever die?"

"Alas! I am very ill."

"Ah, let us talk of that. By Beelzebub! that will lead to just what I wish to speak to you about."

Saying this, the strange being leaped upon the old leather chair, and carried his legs one under the other, after the fashion of the bones which the painters of funeral hangings cross beneath skulls. Then he resumed, in an ironical tone, "See, Master Zacharius, what is going on in this good town of Geneva? They say that your health is failing, that your watches have need of a doctor!"

"Ah, you believe that there is an intimate relation between their existence and mine?" cried Master Zacharius.

"Why, I imagine that these watches have faults, even vices. If these wantons do not preserve a regular conduct, it is right that they should bear the consequences of their irregularity. It seems to me that they have need of reforming a little!"

"What do you call faults?" asked Master Zacharius, reddening at the sarcastic tone in which these words were uttered. "Have they not a right to be proud of their origin?"

"Not too proud, not too proud," replied the little old man. "They bear a celebrated name, and an illustrious signature is graven on their cases, it is true, and theirs is the exclusive privilege of being introduced among the noblest families; but for some time they have become deranged, and you can do nothing about it, Master Zacharius; and the stupidest apprentice in Geneva could prove it to you!"

"To me, to me!" cried Master Zacharius, with a flush of outraged pride.

"To you, Master Zacharius—you, who cannot restore life to your watches!"

"But it is because I have a fever, and so have they also!" replied the old man, as a cold sweat broke out upon him.

"Very well, they will die with you, since you are prevented from imparting a little elasticity to their springs."

"Die! No, for you yourself have said it! I cannot die,—I, the first watchmaker in the world; I, who, by means of these pieces and diverse wheels, have been able to regulate the movement with absolute precision! Have I not subjected time to exact laws, and can I not dispose of it like a despot? Before a sublime genius had disposed regularly these wandering hours, in what vast waste was human destiny plunged? At what certain moment could the acts of life be connected with each other? But you, man or devil, whatever you may be, have never considered the magnificence of my art, which calls every science to its aid! No, no! I, Master Zacharius, cannot die, for, as I have regulated time, time would end with me! It would return to the infinite, whence my genius has rescued it, and it would lose itself irreparably in the gulf of chaos! No, I can no more die than the Creator of this universe, submitted to its laws! I have become his equal, and I have partaken of his power! If God has created eternity, Master Zacharius has created time!"

The old watchmaker now resembled the fallen angel, defiant in the presence of the Creator. The little old man seemed to breathe into him this impious transport.

"Well said, master," he replied. "Beelzebub had less right than you to compare himself with God! Your glory must not perish! So your servant desires to give you the method of controlling these rebellious watches."

"What is it? what is it?" cried Master Zacharius.

"You shall know on the day after that on which you have given me your daughter's hand."

"My Gerande?"

"Herself!"

"My daughter's heart is not free," replied Master Zacharius, who seemed neither astonished nor angry.

"Bah! She is not the least beautiful of watches; but she will end by stopping also——"

"My daughter,—my Gerande! No!"

" Well, return to your watches, Master Zacharius. Adjust and readjust them. Get ready the marriage of your daughter and your apprentice. Temper your springs with your best steel. Bless Aubert and the pretty Gerande. But remember, your watches will never go, and Gerande will not wed Aubert!"

Thereupon the little old man disappeared so quickly that Master Zacharius could not hear six o'clock strike in his breast.

CHAPTER IV
THE CHURCH OF ST. PIERRE

MASTER ZACHARIUS became more feeble in mind and body every day. An unusual excitement, indeed, impelled him to continue his work more eagerly than ever, nor could his daughter entice him from it. From morning till night discontented purchasers besieged the house, and they got access to the old watchmaker himself, who knew not which of them to listen to.

" This watch is too slow, and I cannot succeed in regulating it," said one.

" This," said another, " is absolutely obstinate, and stands still, as did Joshua's sun."

" If it is true," said most of them, " that your health has an influence on that of your watches, Master Zacharius, get well as soon as possible."

The old man gazed at these people with haggard eyes, and only replied by shaking his head, or by a few sad words: " Wait till the first fine weather, my friends. The season is coming which revives existence in wearied bodies. The sun must come to warm us all!"

" A fine thing, if my watches are to be ill through the winter!" said one of the most angry. " Do you know, Master Zacharius, that your name is inscribed in full on their faces? By the Virgin, you do little honor to your signature!"

It happened at last that the old man, abashed by these reproaches, took some pieces of gold from his old trunk, and began to buy back the damaged watches. At news of this, the customers came in a crowd, and the poor watchmaker's money fast melted away; but his honesty remained intact. Gerande warmly praised his delicacy, which was leading him straight towards ruin; and Aubert soon offered his own savings to his master.

Scholastique alone refused to listen to reason on the subject; but her efforts failed to prevent the unwelcome visitors from reaching her master, and from soon departing with some valuable object. Then her chattering was heard in all the streets of the neighborhood, where she had long been known. She eagerly denied the rumors of sorcery and magic on the part of Master Zacharius, which gained currency; but as at bottom she was persuaded of their truth, she said her prayers over and over again to redeem her pious falsehoods.

It had been noticed that for some time the old watchmaker had neglected his religious duties. Time was, when he had accompanied Gerande to church, and had seemed to find in prayer the intellectual charm which it imparts to thoughtful minds, as it is the most sublime exercise of the imagination. This voluntary neglect of holy practices, added to the secret habits of his life, had in some sort confirmed the accusations leveled against his labors. So, with the double purpose of drawing her father back to God and to the world, Gerande resolved to call religion to her aid. She thought that it might give some vitality to his dying soul; but the dogmas of faith and humility had to combat, in the soul of Master Zacharius, an insurmountable pride, and came into collision with that vanity of science which connects everything with itself, without rising to the infinite source whence first principles flow. It was under these circumstances that the young girl undertook her father's conversion, and her influence was so effective that the old watchmaker promised to attend high mass at the Cathedral on the following Sunday.

Old Scholastique could not contain her joy, and at last found irrefutable arguments against the gossiping tongues, which accused her master of impiety. She spoke of it to her neighbors, her friends, her enemies, to those whom she knew not as well as to those whom she knew.

"In faith, we scarcely believe what you tell us, dame Scholastique," they replied; "Master Zacharius has always acted in concert with the devil!"

"You haven't counted, then," replied the old servant, "the fine bells which strike for my master's clocks? How many times they have struck the hours of prayer and the mass!"

"No doubt," they would reply. "But has he not invented machines which go all by themselves, and which actually do the work of a real man?"

"Could a child of the devil," exclaimed dame Scholastique, wrathfully, "have executed the fine iron clock of the château of Andermatt, which the town of Geneva was not rich enough to buy? A pious motto appeared at each hour, and a Christian who obeyed them would have gone straight to Paradise! Is that the work of the devil?"

This masterpiece, made twenty years before, had carried Master Zacharius's fame to its acme; but even then there had been accusations against him of sorcery. At least, the old man's visit to the Cathedral would reduce malicious tongues to silence.

The Sunday so ardently anticipated by Gerande at last arrived. The weather was fine, and the temperature inspiriting. The people of Geneva were passing quietly through the streets, gayly chatting about the return of spring. Gerande, tenderly taking the old man's arm, directed her steps towards the Cathedral, while Scholastique followed behind with the prayer-books. People looked curiously at them as they passed. The old watchmaker permitted himself to be led like a child, or rather like a blind man. The faithful of Saint Pierre were almost frightened when they saw him cross the threshold, and shrank back at his approach.

The chants of high mass were already resounding through the church. Gerande advanced to her accustomed bench, and kneeled with profound and simple reverence. Master Zacharius remained standing beside her.

The ceremonies continued with the majestic solemnity of that pious age, but the old man had no faith. He did not implore the pity of Heaven with cries of anguish of the "Kyrie"; he did not, with the "Gloria in Excelsis," sing the splendors of the celestial heights; the reading of the Testament did not draw him from his materialistic revery, and he forgot to join in the homage of the "Credo." This proud old man remained motionless as insensible and si-

lent as a stone statue; and even at the solemn moment
when the bell announced the miracle of transubstantiation,
he did not bow his head, but gazed directly at the sacred
host which the priest raised above the heads of the faithful. Gerande looked at her father, and a flood of tears
moistened her missal.

At this moment the clock of Saint Pierre struck half
past eleven. Master Zacharius turned quickly towards
this ancient clock which he had regulated and which still
spoke. It seemed to him as if its face was gazing steadily
at him; the figures of the hours shone as if they had been
engraved in lines of fire, and the hands darted forth elec-
tric sparks from their sharp points.

The mass ended. It was customary for the "Angelus"
to be said at noon, and the priests, before leaving the altar,
waited for the clock to strike the hour of twelve. In a
few moments this prayer would ascend to the feet of the
Virgin. But suddenly a harsh noise was heard. Master
Zacharius uttered a piercing cry.

The large hand of the clock, having reached twelve, had
abruptly stopped, and the clock did not strike the hour.

Gerande hastened to her father's aid. He had fallen
down motionless, and they carried him outside the church.
"It is the death-blow!" murmured Gerande, sobbing.

When he had been borne home, Master Zacharius lay
upon his bed utterly crushed. Life seemed only to still
exist on the surface of his body, like the last whiffs of
smoke about a lamp just extinguished.

When he came to his senses, Aubert and Gerande were
leaning over him. At this supreme moment the future
took in his eyes the shape of the present. He saw his
daughter alone, without support. "My son," said he to
Aubert, "I give my daughter to thee."

So saying, he stretched out his hand towards his two
children, who were thus united at his death-bed.

But soon Master Zacharius lifted himself up in a par-
oxysm of rage. The words of the little old man recurred
to his mind. "I do not wish to die!" he cried; "I cannot
die! I, Master Zacharius, ought not to die! My books,—
my accounts!"

He sprang from his bed towards a book in which the
names of his customers and the articles which had been

sold to them, were inscribed. He seized it and rapidly turned over its leaves, and his emaciated thumb fixed itself on one of the pages.

"There!" he cried, "there! this old iron clock, sold to Pittonaccio! It is the only one that has not been returned to me! It still exists,—it goes,—it lives! Ah, I wish for it,—I must find it! I will take such care of it that death will no longer seek me!" And he fainted away.

Aubert and Gerande knelt by the old man's bedside, and prayed together.

CHAPTER V
THE HOUR OF DEATH

SEVERAL days passed, and Master Zacharius, though almost dying, rose from his bed and returned to active life, under a supernatural excitement. He lived by pride. But Gerande did not deceive herself; her father's body and soul were forever lost.

The old man got together his last resources, without thought of those who were dependent upon him. He betrayed an incredible energy, walking, ferreting about, and mumbling strange, incomprehensible words. One morning Gerande went down to his shop. Master Zacharius was not there. She waited for him all day. Master Zacharius did not return.

"Where can he be?" Aubert asked himself. An inspiration suddenly came to his mind. He remembered the last words which Master Zacharius had spoken. The old man only lived now in the old iron clock that had not been returned! Master Zacharius must have gone in search of it. Aubert spoke of this to Gerande.

"Let us look at my father's book," she replied.

They descended to the shop. The book was open on the bench. All the watches or clocks made by the old man, and which had been returned to him out of order, were stricken out, excepting one. "Sold to M. Pittonaccio, an iron clock, with bell and moving figures; sent to his château at Andermatt."

It was this "moral" clock of which Scholastique had spoken with so much enthusiasm.

"My father is there!" cried Gerande.

"Let us hasten thither," replied Aubert. "We may still save him!"

"Not for this life," murmured Gerande, "but at least for the other."

"By the grace of God, Gerande! The château of Andermatt stands in the gorge of the 'Dents-du-Midi,' twenty hours from Geneva. Let us go!"

That very evening Aubert and Gerande, followed by the old servant, set out on foot by the road which skirts Lake Leman. At last, late the next day, they reached the hermitage of Notre-Dame, which is situated at the base of the Dents-du-Midi, six hundred feet above the Rhone. They were nearly dead with fatigue. The hermit received the wanderers as night was falling. They could not have gone another step, and here they must needs rest.

The hermit could give them no news of Master Zacharius. They could scarcely hope to find him still living amid these sad solitudes. The night was dark, the wind howled amid the mountains, and the avalanches roared and thundered down from the summits of the broken crags.

Aubert and Gerande, crouching before the hermit's hearth, told him their melancholy tale. Their mantles, covered with snow, were drying in a corner; and without, the hermit's dog barked lugubriously, and mingled his voice with that of the tempest.

"Pride," said the hermit to his guests, "has lost an angel created for good. It is the obstacle against which the destinies of man strike. You cannot oppose reasoning to pride, the principal of all the vices, since, by its very nature, the proud man refuses to listen to it. It only remains, then, to pray for your father!"

All four knelt down, when the barking of the dog redoubled, and someone knocked at the door of the hermitage. "Open, in the name of the devil!"

The door yielded under the blows, and a disheveled, haggard, ill-clothed man appeared.

"My father!" cried Gerande. It was Master Zacharius.

"Where am I?" said he. "In eternity! Time is ended,—the hours no longer strike,—the hands have stopped!"

"Father!" returned Gerande, with so piteous an emotion that the old man seemed to return to the world of the living.

"Thou here, Gerande?" he cried; "and thou, Aubert? Ah, my dear betrothed ones, you are going to be married in our old church!"

"Father," said Gerande, seizing him by the arm, "come home to Geneva,—come with us!"

"Do not abandon your children!" cried Aubert.

"Why return?" replied the old man, sadly, "to those places which my life has already quitted, and where a part of myself is forever buried?"

"Your soul is not dead!" said the hermit, solemnly.

"My soul? O no,—its wheels are good! I perceive it beating regularly——"

"Your soul is immaterial,—your soul is immortal!" replied the hermit, sternly.

"Yes,—like my glory! But it is shut up in the château of Andermatt, and I wish to see it again!"

The hermit crossed himself; Scholastique became almost inanimate. Aubert held Gerande in his arms.

"The château of Andermatt is inhabited by one who is damned," said the hermit, "one who does not salute the cross of my hermitage."

"My father, go not thither!"

"I want my soul! My soul is mine——"

"Hold him! Hold my father!" cried Gerande.

But the old man had leaped across the threshold, and plunged into the night, crying, "Mine, mine, my soul!"

Gerande, Aubert, and Scholastique hastened after him. They went by difficult paths, across which Master Zacharius sped like a tempest, urged by an irresistible force. The snow raged round them, and mingled its white flakes with the froth of the tumbling torrents.

The château of Andermatt was a ruin even then. A thick, crumbling tower rose above it, and seemed to menace with its downfall the old gables which reared themselves below. The vast piles of jagged stones frowned gloomily to the right. Several dark halls appeared amid the débris, with caved-in ceilings, now become the abode of vipers.

A low and narrow postern, opening upon a ditch choked with rubbish, gave access to the château. No doubt some

margrave, half lord, half brigand, had inherited it; to the
margrave had succeeded bandits or counterfeiters, who
had been hung on the scene of their crime.   The legend
went that on winter nights, Satan came to lead his diabolical
dances on the slope of the deep gorges in which the shadow
of these ruins was engulfed.

But Master Zacharius was not dismayed by their sinister aspect.   He reached the postern.   No one forbade
him to pass.   A spacious and gloomy court presented itself
to his eyes.   He passed along the kind of inclined plane
which conducted to one of the long corridors, the arches of
which seemed to banish daylight from beneath their heavy
springings.   His advance was unresisted.   Gerande, Aubert, and Scholastique closely followed him.

Master Zacharius, as if guided by an irresistible hand,
seemed sure of his way, and strode along with rapid step.
He reached an old worm-eaten door, which fell before his
blows, while the bats described oblique circles around his
head.

An immense hall, better preserved than the rest, was
soon reached.   High sculptured panels, on which larves,
ghouls, and other strange figures seemed to agitate themselves confusedly, covered its walls.   Several long and
narrow windows shivered beneath the bursts of the tempest.

Master Zacharius, on reaching the middle of this hall,
uttered a cry of joy.   On an iron support, fastened to the
wall, stood the clock in which now resided his entire life.
This unequaled masterpiece represented an ancient Roman
church, with its heavy bell-tower, where there was a complete chime for the anthem of the day, the " Angelus,"
the mass, and vespers.   Above the church door, which
opened at the hour of the ceremonies, was placed a " rose,"
in the center of which two hands moved, and the archivolt
of which reproduced the twelve hours of the face sculptured in relief.   Between the door and the rose, just as
Scholastique had said, a maxim, relative to the employ-
ment of every moment of the day, appeared on a copper
plate.   Master Zacharius had regulated this succession of
devices with a really Christian solicitude; the hours of
prayer, of work, of repast, of recreation, and of repose
followed each other according to the religious discipline,

and were infallibly to insure salvation to him who scrupulously observed their commands.

Master Zacharius, intoxicated with joy, went forward
to take possession of the clock, when a frightful roar of
laughter resounded behind him. He turned, and by the
light of a smoky lamp recognized the little old man of
Geneva. "You here?" cried he.

Gerande was afraid. She drew closer to Aubert.

"Good day, Master Zacharius," said the monster.

"Who are you?"

"Signor Pittonaccio, at your service! You have come
to give me your daughter! You have remembered my
words,—'Gerande will not wed Aubert."

The young apprentice rushed upon Pittonaccio, who
escaped from him like a shadow.

"Stop, Aubert!" cried Master Zacharius.

"Good night," said Pittonaccio; and he disappeared.

"My father, let us fly from this hateful place!" cried
Gerande. "My father!"

Master Zacharius was no longer there. He was pursuing the phantom of Pittonaccio across the rickety corridors. Scholastique, Gerande, and Aubert remained,
speechless and fainting, in the large gloomy hall. The
young girl had fallen upon a stone seat; the old servant
knelt beside her and prayed; Aubert remained erect
watching his betrothed. Pale lights wandered in the
darkness, and the silence was only broken by the movements
of the little animals which range among old wood, and
the noise of which marks the hours of "the clock of
death."

When daylight came, they ventured upon the endless
staircase which wound beneath these ruined masses; for
two hours they wandered thus, without meeting a living
soul, and hearing only a far-off echo responding to their
cries. Sometimes they found themselves buried a hundred
feet below the ground, and sometimes they reached places
whence they could overlook the surrounding mountains.

Chance brought them at last back again to the vast hall,
which had sheltered them during this night of anguish.
It was no longer empty. Master Zacharius and Pittonaccio were talking there together, the one upright and rigid
as a corpse, the other crouching over a marble table.

Master Zacharius, when he perceived Gerande, went forward and took her by the hand, and led her towards Pittonaccio, saying, "Behold your lord and master, my daughter. Gerande, behold your husband!"

Gerande shuddered from head to foot.

"Never!" cried Aubert, "for she is my betrothed."

"Never!" responded Gerande, like a plaintive echo.

Pittonaccio began to laugh.

"You wish me to die, then?" exclaimed the old man. "There, in that clock, the last which goes of all which have gone from my hands, my life is shut up; and this man tells me, 'When I have thy daughter, this clock shall belong to thee.' And this man will not adjust it. He can break it, and plunge me into chaos. Ah, my daughter, you no longer love me!"

"My father!" murmured Gerande, recovering consciousness.

"If you knew what I have suffered, far away from this principle of my existence!" resumed the old man. "Perhaps its springs were left to wear out, its wheels to get clogged. But now, in my own hands, I can nourish this health so dear, for I must not die,—I, the great watchmaker of Geneva. Look, my daughter, how these hands advance with certain step. See, five o'clock is about to strike. Listen well, and look at the maxim which is about to be revealed."

Five o'clock struck with a noise which resounded sadly in Gerande's soul, and these words appeared in red letters:

"YOU MUST EAT OF THE FRUITS OF THE TREE OF SCIENCE."

Aubert and Gerande looked at each other stupefied. These were no longer the pious sayings of the Catholic watchmaker. The breath of Satan must have passed there. But Zacharius paid no attention to this, and resumed: "Dost thou hear, my Gerande? I live, I still live! Listen to my breathing,—see the blood circulating in my veins! No, thou wouldst not kill thy father, and thou wilt accept this man for thy husband, so that I may become immortal, and at last attain the power of God!"

At these blasphemous words old Scholastique crossed herself, and Pittonaccio laughed aloud with joy.

"And then, Gerande, thou wilt be happy with him. See this man,—he is Time! Thy existence will be regulated with absolute precision. Gerande, since I gave thee life, give life to thy father!"

"Gerande," murmured Aubert, "I am thy betrothed."

"He is my father!" replied Gerande, fainting.

"She is thine!" said Master Zacharius. "Pittonaccio, thou wilt keep thy promise!"

"Here is the key of the clock," replied the horrible man.

Master Zacharius seized the long key, which resembled an uncoiled snake, and ran to the clock, which he hastened to wind up with fantastic rapidity. The creaking of the spring jarred upon the nerves. The old watchmaker wound and wound the key, without stopping a moment, and it seemed as if the movement were beyond his control. He wound more and more quickly, with strange contortions, until he fell from sheer weariness.

"There it is, wound up for a century!" he cried.

Aubert rushed from the hall as if he were mad. After long wandering, he found the outlet of the hateful château, and hastened into the open air. He returned to the hermitage of Notre-Dame, and talked so desperately to the holy recluse, that the latter consented to return with him to the chateau of Andermatt.

Master Zacharius had not left the hall. He ran every moment to listen to the regular beating of the old clock. Meanwhile the clock had struck, and to Scholastique's great terror, these words had appeared on the silver face:

"MAN OUGHT TO BECOME THE EQUAL OF GOD."

The old man had not only not been shocked by these impious maxims, but read them deliriously, and was pleased with these thoughts of pride, while Pittonaccio kept close by him.

The marriage-contract was to be signed at midnight. Gerande, almost unconscious, saw or heard nothing. The silence was only broken by the old man's words, and the chuckling of Pittonaccio.

Eleven o'clock struck.   Master Zacharius read in a loud voice:

" MAN SHOULD BE THE SLAVE OF SCIENCE, AND SACRIFICE TO IT RELATIVES AND FAMILY."

"Yes!" he cried, "there is nothing but science in this world!"

The hands slipped over the face of the clock with the hiss of a serpent, and the movement beat with accelerated strokes. Master Zacharius no longer spoke. He had fallen to the floor, he rattled, and from his oppressed bosom came only these half-broken words, "Life—science!"

The scene had now two new witnesses, the hermit and Aubert. Master Zacharius lay upon the floor; Gerande was praying beside him, more dead than alive. Of a sudden a dry, hard noise was heard, proceeding from the striking-apparatus.

Master Zacharius sprang up.   "Midnight!" he cried.

The hermit stretched out his hand towards the old watchmaker,—and midnight did not sound.

Master Zacharius uttered a terrible cry, when these words appeared:

" WHOEVER SHALL ATTEMPT TO MAKE HIMSELF THE EQUAL OF GOD SHALL BE FOREVER DAMNED!"

The old clock burst with a noise like thunder, and the spring, escaping, leaped across the hall with a thousand fantastic contortions; the old man rose, ran after it, trying in vain to seize it, and exclaiming, "My soul,—my soul!"

The spring bounded before him, first on one side, then on the other, and he could not reach it.

At last Pittonaccio seized it, and, uttering a horrible blasphemy, ingulfed himself in the earth.

Master Zacharius fell over.   He was dead.

The old watchmaker was buried in the midst of the peaks of Andermatt.

Then Aubert and Gerande returned to Geneva, and during the long life which God accorded to them, they imposed it on themselves to redeem by prayer the soul of the castaway of science.

THE END

A Winter Amid the Ice

OR

The Cruise of the Jeune Hardie

A Winter Amid the Ice

CHAPTER I
THE BLACK FLAG

T HE curé of the ancient church of Dunkirk rose at five o'clock on the 12th of May, 18—, to perform, according to his custom, low mass for a few pious sinners.

Attired in his priestly robes, he was ready for the altar, when a man entered the sacristy, at once joyous and frightened. He was a sailor of some sixty years, but still vigorous and sturdy, with an open, honest countenance.

"Monsieur the curé," said he, "stop a moment, please."

"What do you want so early in the morning, Jean Cornbutte?" asked the curé.

"Want? Why, to embrace you in my arms, i' faith!"

"Well, after the mass at which you are going to be present——"

"The mass?" returned the old sailor, laughing. "Do you think you are going to say your mass now, and that I will let you do so?"

"And why should I not say my mass?" asked the curé. "Explain yourself. The third bell has sounded——"

"Whether it has or not," replied Jean Cornbutte, "it will sound many times to-day, monsieur, for you have promised me that you will bless, with your own hands, the marriage of my son Louis and my niece Marie!"

"He has arrived, then," said the curé joyfully.

"It is nearly the same thing," replied Cornbutte, rubbing his hands. "Our brig was signaled from the lookout at sunrise,—our brig, which you yourself christened by the good name of the ' Jeune-Hardie ' ! "

"I congratulate you with all my heart, Cornbutte," said the curé. "I remember our agreement. The vicar will take my place, and I will put myself at your disposal against your dear son's arrival."

55

" And I promise you that he will not make you fast long,"
replied the sailor. " You have published the banns, and you
will only have to absolve him from the sins he may have
committed between sky and water, in the Northern Ocean.
It is a grand idea, the marriage celebrated the very day he
arrives, and my son Louis shall leave his ship to go at once
to the church."

" Go, then, and arrange everything, Cornbutte."

" I fly, monsieur the curé.   Good-morning!"

The sailor hastened with rapid steps to his house, which
stood on the quay, whence could be seen the Northern Ocean,
of which he seemed so proud.

Jean Cornbutte had amassed a comfortable sum at his
calling.   After having long commanded the vessels of a rich
ship-owner of Havre, he had settled down in his native town,
where he had caused the brig *Jeune-Hardie* to be constructed
at his own expense.   Several successful voyages had been
made in the North, and the ship always found a good sale
for its cargoes of wood, iron, and tar.   Jean Cornbutte
then gave up the command of her to his son Louis, a fine
sailor of thirty, who, according to all the coasting captains,
was the boldest mariner in Dunkirk.

Louis Cornbutte had gone away deeply attached to Marie,
his father's niece, who found the time of his absence very
long and weary.   Marie was scarcely twenty.   She was a
pretty Flemish girl, with some Dutch blood in her veins.
Her mother, when she was dying, had confided her to her
brother, Jean Cornbutte.   The brave old sailor loved her as
a daughter, and saw in her proposed union with Louis a
source of real and durable happiness.

The arrival of the ship, already signaled off the coast,
completed an important business operation, from which Jean
Cornbutte expected large profits.   The *Jeune-Hardie,* which
had left three months before, came last from Bodoe, on the
west coast of Norway, and had made a quick voyage thence.

On returning home, Jean Cornbutte found the whole
house alive.   Marie, with radiant face, had assumed her
wedding-dress.   " I hope the ship will not arrive before we
are ready!" she said.

" Hurry, little one," replied Jean Cornbutte, " for the
wind is north, and she sails well, you know."

" Have our friends been told uncle?" asked Marie.

" They have."

" The notary, and the curé? "

" Rest easy. You alone are keeping us waiting."

At this moment Clerbaut, an old crony, came in. " Well, old Cornbutte," cried he, " here's luck! Your ship has arrived at the very moment that the government has decided to contract for a large quantity of wood for the navy! "

" What is that to me? " replied Jean Cornbutte. " What care I for the government? "

" You see, Monsieur Clerbaut," said Marie, " one thing only absorbs us,—Louis's return."

" I don't dispute that," replied Clerbaut. " But—in short —this purchase of wood——"

" And you shall be at the wedding," replied Jean Cornbutte, interrupting the merchant, and shaking his hand as if he would crush it.

" This purchase of wood——"

" And with all our friends, landsmen and seamen, Clerbaut. I have already informed everybody, and I shall invite the whole crew of the ship."

" And shall we go and await them on the pier? " asked Marie.

" Indeed we will," replied Jean Cornbutte. " We will defile, two by two, with the violins at the head."

Jean Cornbutte's invited guests soon arrived. Though it was very early, not a single one failed to appear. All congratulated the honest old sailor whom they loved. Meanwhile Marie, kneeling down, changed her prayers to God into thanksgivings. She soon returned, lovely and decked out, to the company; all the women kissed her, while the men vigorously grasped her by the hand.

It was a curious sight to see this joyous group taking its way, at sunrise, towards the sea. The news of the ship's arrival had spread through the port, and many heads, in nightcaps, appeared at windows and half-opened doors. Compliments and pleasant nods came from every side.

The party reached the pier in the midst of a concert of praise and blessings. The weather was magnificent, and the sun seemed to take part in the festivity. A fresh north wind made the waves foam; and some fishing-smacks, their sails trimmed for leaving port, streaked the sea with their rapid wakes between the breakwaters.

The two piers of Dunkirk stretch far out into the sea. The wedding-party occupied the whole width of the northern pier, and soon reached a small house situated at its extremity, inhabited by the harbor-master. The wind freshened, and the *Jeune-Hardie* ran swiftly under her topsails, mizzen, brigantine, gallant, and royal. Jean Cornbutte, spyglass in hand, responded merrily to the questions of his friends.

"See my ship!" he cried; "clean and steady as if she had been rigged at Dunkirk! Not a bit of damage done, —not a rope wanting!"

"Do you see your son, the captain?" asked one.

"No, not yet. Why, he's at his business!"

"Why doesn't he run up his flag?" asked Clerbaut.

"I scarcely know. He has a reason for it, I have no doubt."

"Your spy-glass, uncle?" said Marie, taking it from him. "I want to be the first to see him."

"But he is my son, mademoiselle!"

"He has been your son for thirty years," answered the young girl, laughing, "and he has only been my betrothed for two!"

The *Jeune-Hardie* was now entirely visible. Already the crew were preparing to cast anchor. The upper sails had been reefed. The sailors who were among the rigging might be recognized. But neither Marie nor Jean Cornbutte had yet been able to wave their hands at the captain of the ship.

"There's the mate, André Vasling," cried Clerbaut.

"There's Fidèle, the carpenter," said another.

"And our friend Penellan," said a third, saluting the sailor named.

The *Jeune-Hardie* was only three cables' lengths from the shore, when a black flag ascended to the gaff of the brigantine. There was mourning on board the boat. A shudder of terror seized the party and the heart of the young girl.

The ship sadly swayed into port, and an icy silence reigned on its deck. Soon it had passed the end of the pier. Marie, Jean Cornbutte, and all their friends hurried towards the quay at which she was to anchor, and in a moment found themselves on board.

" My son!" said Jean Cornbutte.

The sailors, with uncovered heads, pointed to the mourning flag. Marie uttered a cry of anguish, and fell into old Cornbutte's arms.

André Vasling had brought back the *Jeune-Hardie*, but Louis Cornbutte, Marie's betrothed, was not on board.

CHAPTER II
JEAN CORNBUTTE'S PROJECT

As soon as the young girl, confided to the care of the sympathizing friends, had left the ship, André Vasling, the mate, apprised Jean Cornbutte of the dreadful event which had deprived him of his son, narrated in the ship's journal as follows:—

" Near the Maëlstrom, on the 26th of April, bad weather and south-west winds. Perceived signals of distress made by a schooner to the leeward. This schooner, deprived of its mizzen-mast, was running towards the whirlpool, under bare poles. Captain Louis Cornbutte, seeing that this vessel was hastening into danger, resolved to board her. Despite the remonstrances of his crew, he had the long-boat lowered into the sea, and got into it, with the sailor Courtois and the helmsman Pierre Nouquet The crew watched them until they disappeared in the fog. Night came on. The sea became more and more boisterous. The *Jeune-Hardie* was in danger of being engulfed by the Maëlstrom. She was obliged to fly before the wind. For several days she hovered near the place of the disaster. The long-boat, the schooner, Captain Louis, and the two sailors did not reappear. André Vasling then called the crew together, took command of the ship, and set sail for Dunkirk."

After reading this dry narrative, Jean Cornbutte wept for a long time; if he had any consolation, it was that his son had died in attempting to save his fellow-men. Then the poor father left the ship, the sight of which made him wretched, and returned to his desolate home.

The sad news soon spread throughout Dunkirk. The many friends of the old sailor came to bring him their sincere sympathy. Then the sailors of the *Jeune-Hardie* gave a more particular account of the event, and André Vasling

told Marie, at great length, of the devotion of her betrothed
to the last.

When he ceased weeping, Jean Cornbutte, the next day
after the ship's arrival, said, " Are you very sure, Andre,
that my son has perished?"

" Alas, yes, Monsieur Jean," replied the mate.

" And you made all possible search for him? "

" All, Monsieur Cornbutte. But it is unhappily but too
certain that he and the two sailors were sucked down in
the whirlpool of the Maelstrom."

" Would you like, André, to keep the second command
of the ship? "

" That will depend upon the captain, Monsieur Jean."

" I shall be the captain," replied the old sailor. " I am
going to discharge the cargo with all speed, make up my
crew, and sail in search of my son."

" Your son is dead! " said André obstinately.

" It is possible, André," replied Jean Cornbutte sharply,
" but it is also possible that he saved himself. I am going
to rummage all the ports of Norway, and when I am fully
convinced that I shall never see him again, I will return here
to die!"

André Vasling, seeing that this decision was irrevocable,
did not insist further, but went away.

Jean Cornbutte at once told his niece of his intention, and
he saw a few rays of hope glisten across her tears. It had
not seemed to the young girl that her lover's death could
be doubtful; but when this new hope entered her heart, she
embraced it without reserve.

The old sailor determined that the *Jeune-Hardie* should
put to sea without delay. The solidly built ship had no
need of repairs. Jean Cornbutte gave his sailors notice
that if they wished to re-embark, no change in the crew
would be made. He alone replaced his son in the command
of the brig. None of the comrades of Louis Cornbutte
failed to respond to his call, and there were hardy tars
among them,—Alaine Turquiette, Fidèle Misonne, the carpenter, Penellan the Breton, who replaced Pierre Nouquet
as helmsman, and Gradlin, Aupic, and Gervique, courageous
and well-tried mariners.

Jean again offered André Vasling his old rank
on board. The first mate was an able officer who had

proved his skill in bringing the *Jeune-Hardie* into port. Yet, from what motive could not be told, André made some difficulties and asked time for reflection.

"As you will, André," replied Cornbutte. "Only remember that if you accept, you will be welcome."

Jean had a devoted sailor in Penellan the Breton, who had long been his fellow-voyager. In times gone by, little Marie was wont to pass the long winter evenings in the helmsman's arms, when he was on shore. He felt a fatherly friendship for her, and she had for him an affection quite filial. Penellan hastened the fitting out of the ship with all his energy, all the more because, according to his opinion, André Vasling had not perhaps made every effort possible to find the castaways, although he was excusable from the responsibility which weighed upon him as captain.

Within a week the *Jeune-Hardie* was ready to put to sea. Instead of merchandise, she was completely provided with salt meats, biscuits, barrels of flour, potatoes, pork, wine, brandy, coffee, tea, and tobacco.

The departure was fixed for the 22nd of May. On the evening before, André Vasling, who had not yet given his answer to Jean Cornbutte, came to his house. He was still undecided, and did not know which course to take.

Jean was not at home, though the house door was open. André went into the passage, next to Marie's chamber, where the sound of an animated conversation struck his ear. He listened attentively, and recognized the voices of Penellan and Marie.

The discussion had no doubt been going on for some time, for the young girl seemed to be stoutly opposing what the Breton sailor said.

"How old is my uncle Cornbutte?" said Marie.

"Something about sixty years," replied Penellan.

"Well, is he not going to brave danger to find his son?"

"Our captain is still a sturdy man," returned the sailor. "He has a body of oak and muscles as hard as a spare spar. So I am not afraid to have him go to sea again!"

"My good Penellan," said Marie, "one is strong when one loves! Besides, I have full confidence in the aid of Heaven. You understand me, and will help me."

"No!" said Penellan. "It is impossible, Marie. Who knows whither we shall drift, or what we must suffer? How many vigorous men have I seen lose their lives in these seas!"

"Penellan," returned the young girl, "if you refuse me, I shall believe that you do not love me any longer."

André Vasling guessed the young girl's resolution. He reflected a moment, and his course was determined on.

"Jean Cornbutte," said he, advancing towards the old sailor, who now entered, "I will go with you. The cause of my hesitation has disappeared, and you may count upon my devotion."

"I have never doubted you, André Vasling," replied Jean Cornbutte, grasping him by the hand. "Marie, my child!" he added, calling in a loud voice.

Marie and Penellan made their appearance.

"We shall set sail to-morrow at daybreak, with the outgoing tide," said Jean. "My poor Marie, this is the last evening that we shall pass together."

"Uncle!" cried Marie, throwing herself into his arms.

"Marie, by the help of God, I will bring your lover back."

"Yes, we will find Louis," added André Vasling.

"You are going with us, then?" asked Penellan quickly.

"Yes, Penellan, André Vasling is to be my first mate," answered Jean.

"Oh, oh!" ejaculated the Breton, in a singular tone.

"His advice will be useful, for he is able and enterprising."

"And yourself, captain," said André. "You will set us all a good example, for you have still as much vigor as experience."

"Well, my friends, good-by till to-morrow. Go on board and make the final arrangements. Good-by, André; good-by, Penellan."

The mate and the sailor went out together, and Jean and Marie remained alone. Many bitter tears were shed during that sad evening. Jean Cornbutte, seeing Marie so wretched, resolved to spare her the pain of separation by leaving the house on the morrow without her knowledge. So he gave her a last kiss that evening, and at three o'clock next morning was up and away.

The departure of the brig had attracted all the old sailor's friends to the pier. The curé, who was to have blessed Marie's union with Louis, came to give a last benediction on the ship. Rough grasps of the hand were silently exchanged, and Jean went on board.

The crew were all there. André Vasling gave the last orders. The sails were spread, and the brig rapidly passed out under a stiff northwest breeze, whilst the curé, upright in the midst of the kneeling spectators, committed the vessel to the hands of God. " Whither goes this ship? She follows the perilous route upon which so many castaways have been lost! She has no certain destination. She must expect every peril, and be able to brave them without hesitating. God alone knows where it will be her fate to anchor. May God guide her!"

CHAPTER III
A RAY OF HOPE

At that time of the year the season was favorable, and the crew might hope promptly to reach the scene of the shipwreck.

Jean Cornbutte's plan was naturally traced out. He counted on stopping at the Faroë Islands, whither the north wind might have carried the castaways; then, if he was convinced that they had not been received in any of the ports of that locality, he would continue his search beyond the Northern Ocean, ransack the whole western coast of Norway as far as Bodoë, the place nearest the scene of the shipwreck; and, if necessary, farther still.

André Vasling thought, contrary to the captain's opinion, that the coast of Iceland should be explored; but Penellan observed that, at the time of the catastrophe, the gale came from the west; which, while it gave hope that the unfortunates had not been forced towards the gulf of the Maëlstrom, gave ground for supposing that they might have been thrown on the Norwegian coast.

It was determined, then, that this coast should be followed as closely as possible, so as to recognize any traces of them that might appear.

The day after sailing, Jean Cornbutte, intent upon a map, was absorbed in reflection, when a small hand touched his shoulder, and a soft voice said in his ear, " Have good courage, uncle."

He turned, and was stupefied. Marie embraced him.

"Marie, my daughter, on board!" he cried.

"The wife may well go in search of her husband, when the father embarks to save his child."

"Unhappy Marie! How wilt thou support our fatigues! Dost know thy presence may retard our search?"

"No, uncle, for I am strong."

"Who knows whither we shall be forced to go, Marie? Look at this map. We are approaching places dangerous even for us sailors, hardened though we are to the difficulties of the sea. And thou, frail child?"

"But, uncle, I come from a family of sailors. I am used to stories of combats and tempests. I am with you and my old friend Penellan!"

"Penellan! It was he who concealed you on board?"

"Yes, uncle; but only when he saw that I was determined to come without his help."

"Penellan!" cried Jean. Penellan entered.

"It is not possible to undo what you have done, Penellan; but remember that you are responsible for Marie's life."

"Rest easy, captain," replied Penellan. "The little one has force and courage, and will be our guardian angel. And then, captain, you know it is my theory, that all in this world happens for the best."

The young girl was installed in a cabin, which the sailors soon got ready for her, and which they made as comfortable as possible.

A week later the *Jeune-Hardie* stopped at the Faroë Islands, but the most minute search was fruitless. No wreck, or fragments of a ship had come upon these coasts. The brig resumed its voyage, after a stay of ten days, about the 10th of June. The sea was calm, and the winds were favorable. The ship sped rapidly towards the Norwegian coast, which it explored without better result.

Jean Cornbutte determined to proceed to Bodoë. Perhaps he would there learn the name of the shipwrecked schooner to succor which Louis and the sailors had sacrificed themselves.

On the 30th of June the brig cast anchor in that port.

The authorities of Bodoë gave Jean Cornbutte a bottle found on the coast, which contained a document bearing these words: "This 26th April, on board the *Froöern*, after being accosted by the long-boat of the *Jeune-Hardie,* we were drawn by the currents towards the ice. God have pity on us!"

Jean Cornbutte's first impulse was to thank Heaven. He thought himself on his son's track. The *Froöern* was a Norwegian sloop of which there had been no news, but which had evidently been drawn northward.

Not a day was to be lost. The *Jeune-Hardie* was at once put in condition to brave the perils of the polar seas. Fidèle Misonne, the carpenter, carefully examined her, and assured himself that her solid construction might resist the shock of the ice-masses.

Penellan, who had already engaged in whale-fishing in the arctic waters, took care that woolen and fur coverings, many sealskin moccasins, and wood for the making of sledges with which to cross the ice-fields were put on board. The amount of provisions was increased, and spirits and charcoal were added; for it might be that they would have to winter at some point on the Greenland coast. They also procured, with much difficulty and at a high price, a quantity of lemons, for preventing or curing the scurvy, that terrible disease which decimates crews in the icy regions. The ship's hold was filled with salt meat, biscuits, brandy, etc., as the steward's room no longer sufficed. They provided themselves, also, with a large quantity of "pemmican," an Indian preparation which concentrates much nutrition within a small volume.

By order of the captain, some saws were put on board for cutting the ice-fields, as well as picks and wedges for separating them. The captain determined to procure some dogs to be used for drawing the sledges on the Greenland coast.

The whole crew was engaged in these preparations, and displayed great activity. The sailors Aupic, Gervique, and Gradlin zealously obeyed Penellan's orders; and he admonished them not to accustom themselves to woolen garments, though the temperature in this latitude, situated just beyond the polar circle, was very low.

Penellan, though he said nothing, narrowly watched every action of André Vasling. This man was Dutch by birth, came from no one knew whither, but was at least a good sailor, having made two voyages on board the *Jeune-Hardie.*

Penellan would not as yet accuse him of anything, unless it was that he kept near Marie too constantly, but he did not let him out of his sight.

Thanks to the energy of the crew, the brig was equipped by the 16th of July, a fortnight after its arrival at Bodoë. It was then the favorable season for attempting explorations in the Arctic Seas. The thaw had been going on for two months, and the search might be carried farther north. The *Jeune-Hardie* set sail, and directed her way towards Cape Brewster, on the eastern coast of Greenland, near the 70th degree of latitude.

CHAPTER IV
IN THE PASSES

ABOUT the 23rd of July a reflection, raised above the sea, announced the presence of the first icebergs, which, emerging from Davis's Straits, advanced into the ocean. From this moment a vigilant watch was ordered to the look-out men, for it was important not to come into collision with these enormous masses.

The crew was divided into two watches. The first was composed of Fidele Misonne, Gradlin, and Gervique; and the second of André Vasling, Aupic, and Penellan. These watches were to last only two hours, for in those cold regions a man's strength is diminished one-half. Though the *Jeune-Hardie* was not yet beyond the 63rd degree of latitude, the thermometer already stood at nine degrees centigrade below zero.

Rain and snow often fell abundantly. On fair days, when the wind was not too violent, Marie remained on deck, and her eyes became accustomed to the uncouth scenes of the Polar Seas.

On the 1st of August she was talking with her uncle, Penellan, and André Vasling. The ship was then entering a channel three miles wide, across which broken masses of ice were rapidly descending southwards.

" When shall we see land? " asked the young girl.

" In four days at the latest," replied Jean Cornbutte.

" But shall we find there fresh traces of Louis? "

" Perhaps so, my daughter; but I fear that we are still

far from the end of our voyage. It is to be feared that the
Froöern was driven farther northward."

"That may be," added André Vasling, "for the squall
which separated us from the Norwegian coast lasted three
days, and in three days a ship makes good headway when
it is no longer able to resist the wind."

"Permit me to tell you, Monsieur Vasling," replied Penellan, "that that was in April, that the thaw had not then begun, and that therefore the *Froöern* must have been soon
arrested by the ice."

"And no doubt dashed into a thousand pieces," said the
mate, "as her crew could not manage her."

"But these ice-fields," returned Penellan, "gave her an
easy means of reaching land, from which she could not have
been far distant."

"Let us hope so," said Jean Cornbutte, interrupting the
discussion, which was daily renewed between the mate and
the helmsman. "I think we shall see land before long."

"There it is!" cried Marie. "See those mountains!"

"No, my child," replied her uncle. "Those are mountains of ice, the first we have met with. They would shat-
ter us like glass if we got entangled between them. Penellan and Vasling, overlook the men."

These floating masses, more than fifty of which now appeared at the horizon, came nearer and nearer to the brig
Penellan took the helm, and Jean Cornbutte, mounted on
the gallant, indicated the route to take.

Towards evening the brig was entirely surrounded by
these moving rocks, the crushing force of which is irresistible. It was necessary, then, to cross this fleet of mountains, for prudence prompted them to keep straight ahead.
Another difficulty was added to these perils. The direction
of the ship could not be accurately determined, as all the
surrounding points constantly changed position, and thus
failed to afford a fixed perspective. The darkness soon increased with the fog. Marie descended to her cabin, and
the whole crew, by the captain's orders, remained on deck.
They were armed with long boat-poles, with iron spikes, to
preserve the ship from collision with the ice.

The ship soon entered a strait so narrow that often the
ends of her yards were grazed by the drifting mountains,
and her booms seemed about to be driven in. They were

even forced to trim the mainyard so as to touch the shrouds.
Happily these precautions did not deprive the vessel of any
of its speed, for the wind could only reach the upper sails,
and these sufficed to carry her forward rapidly. Thanks to
her slender hull, she passed through these valleys, which
were filled with whirlpools of rain, whilst the icebergs
crushed against each other with sharp cracking and splitting.

Jean Cornbutte returned to the deck. His eyes could not
penetrate the surrounding darkness. It became necessary
to furl the upper sails, for the ship threatened to ground,
and if she did so she was lost.

"Cursed voyage!" growled André Vasling among the
sailors, who, forward, were avoiding the most menacing
ice-blocks with their boat-hooks.

"Truly, if we escape we shall owe a fine candle to Our
Lady of the Ice!" replied Aupic.

"Who knows how many floating mountains we have got
to pass through yet?" added the mate.

"And who can guess what we shall find beyond them?"
replied the sailor.

"Don't talk so much, prattler," said Gervique, "and look
out on your side. When we have got by them, it'll be time
to grumble. Look out for your boat-hook!"

At this moment an enormous block of ice, in the narrow
strait through which the brig was passing, came rapidly
down upon her, and it seemed impossible to avoid it, for it
barred the whole width of the channel, and the brig could
not heave-to.

"Do you feel the tiller?" asked Cornbutte of Penellan.

"No, captain. The ship does not answer the helm."

"Ohé, boys!" cried the captain to the crew; "don't be
afraid, brace your hooks against the gunwale."

The block was nearly sixty feet high, and if it threw itself
upon the brig she would be crushed. There was an unde-
finable moment of suspense, and the crew retreated back-
ward, abandoning their posts despite the captain's orders.

But at the instant when the block was not more than half
a cable's length from the *Jeune-Hardie,* a dull sound was
heard, and a veritable waterspout fell upon the bow of the
vessel, which then rose on the back of an enormous billow.

The sailors uttered a cry of terror; but when they looked
before them the block had disappeared, the passage was

free, and beyond an immense plain of water, illumined by the rays of the declining sun, assured them of an easy navigation.

"All's well!" cried Penellan. "Let's trim our topsails and mizzen!"

An incident very common in those parts had just occurred. When these masses are detached from one another in the thawing season, they float in a perfect equilibrium; but on reaching the ocean, where the water is relatively warmer, they are speedily undermined at the base, which melts little by little, and which is also shaken by the shock of other ice-masses. A moment comes when the center of gravity of these masses is displaced, and then they are completely overturned. Only, if this block had turned over two minutes later, it would have fallen on the brig and carried her down in its fall.

CHAPTER V
LIVERPOOL ISLAND

ON the 3rd of August the brig confronted immovable and united ice-masses. The passages were seldom more than a cable's length in width, and the ship was forced to make many turnings, which sometimes placed her heading the wind.

Penellan watched over Marie with paternal care, and, despite the cold, prevailed upon her to spend two or three hours every day on deck, for exercise had become one of the indispensable conditions of health.

Marie's courage did not falter. She even comforted the sailors with her cheerful talk, and all of them became warmly attached to her. André Vasling showed himself more attentive than ever, and seized every occasion to be in her company; but the young girl, with a sort of presentiment, accepted his services with some coldness. It may be easily conjectured that André's conversation referred more to the future than to the present, and that he did not conceal the slight probability there was of saving the castaways. He was convinced that they were lost, and the young girl ought thenceforth to confide her existence to someone else.

Marie had not as yet comprehended André's designs, for,

to his great disgust, he could never find an opportunity to talk long with her alone. Penellan had always an excuse for interfering, and destroying the effect of André's words by the hopeful opinions he expressed.

Marie, meanwhile, did not remain idle. Acting on the helmsman's advice, she set to work on her winter garments; for it was necessary that she should completely change her clothing. The cut of her dresses was not suitable for these cold latitudes. She made, therefore, a sort of furred pantaloons, the ends of which were lined with seal-skin; and her narrow skirts came only to her knees, so as not to be in contact with the layers of snow with which the winter would cover the ice-fields. A fur mantle, fitting closely to the figure and supplied with a hood, protected the upper part of her body.

In the intervals of their work, the sailors, too, prepared clothing with which to shelter themselves from the cold. They made a quantity of high seal-skin boots, with which to cross the snow during their explorations. They worked thus all the time that the navigation in the straits lasted.

André Vasling, who was an excellent shot, several times brought down aquatic birds with his gun; innumerable flocks of these were always careering about the ship. A kind of eider-duck provided the crew with very palatable food, which relieved the monotony of the salt meat.

At last the brig came in sight of Cape Brewster. A long-boat was put to sea. Jean Cornbutte and Penellan reached the coast, which was entirely deserted.

The ship at once directed its course towards Liverpool Island, discovered in 1821 by Captain Scoresby, and the crew gave a hearty cheer when they saw the natives running along the shore. Communication was speedily established with them, thanks to Penellan's knowledge of a few words of their language, and some phrases which the natives themselves had learnt of the whalers who frequented those parts.

These Greenlanders were small and squat; they were not more than four feet ten inches high; they had red, round faces, and low foreheads; their hair, flat and black, fell over their shoulders; their teeth were decayed, and they seemed to be affected by the sort of leprosy which is peculiar to ichthyophagous tribes.

In exchange for pieces of iron and brass, of which they are extremely covetous, these poor creatures brought bear furs, the skins of sea-calves, sea-dogs, sea-wolves, and all the animals generally known as seals. Jean Cornbutte obtained these at a low price, and they were certain to become most useful.

The captain then made the natives understand that he was in search of a shipwrecked vessel, and asked them if they had heard of it. One of them immediately drew something like a ship on the snow, and indicated that a vessel of that sort had been carried northward three months before: he also managed to make it understood that the thaw and breaking up of the ice-fields had prevented the Greenlanders from going in search of it; and, indeed, their very light canoes, which they managed with paddles, could not go to sea at that time.

This news, though meager, restored hope to the hearts of the sailors, and Jean Cornbutte had no difficulty in persuading them to advance farther in the polar seas.

Before quitting Liverpool Island, the captain purchased a pack of six Esquimaux dogs, which were soon acclimatized on board. The ship weighed anchor on the morning of the 10th of August, and sailed north under a brisk wind.

The longest days of the year had now arrived; that is, the sun, in these high latitudes, did not set, and reached the highest point of the spirals which it described above the horizon. This total absence of night was not, however, very apparent, for the fog, rain, and snow sometimes enveloped the ship in real darkness.

Jean Cornbutte, who was resolved to advance as far as possible, began to take measures of health. The space between decks was securely enclosed, and every morning care was taken to ventilate it with fresh air. The stoves were installed, and the pipes so disposed as to yield as much heat as possible. The sailors were advised to wear only one woolen shirt over their cotton shirts, and to hermetically close their seal cloaks. The fires were not yet lighted, for it was important to reserve the wood and charcoal for the most intense cold. Warm beverages, such as coffee and tea, were regularly distributed to the sailors morning and evening; and as it was important to live on meat, they shot ducks and teal, which abounded in these parts.

Jean Cornbutte also placed at the summit of the main-
mast a "crow's nest," a sort of cask open at one end, in
which a look-out remained constantly, to observe the ice-
fields.

Two days after the brig had lost sight of Liverpool Island
the temperature became suddenly colder under the influence
of a dry wind. Some indications of winter were perceived.
The ship had not a moment to lose, for soon the way would
be entirely closed to her. She advanced across the straits,
among which lay ice-plains thirty feet thick.

On the morning of the 3rd of September the *Jeune-Hardie*
reached the head of Gael-Hamkes Bay. Land was then
thirty miles to the leeward. It was the first time that the
brig had stopped before a mass of ice which offered no outlet, and which was at least a mile wide. The saws must
now be used to cut the ice. Penellan, Aupic, Gradlin, and
Turquiette were chosen to work the saws, which had been
carried outside the ship. The direction of the cutting was
so determined that the current might carry off the pieces
detached from the mass. The whole crew worked at this
task for nearly twenty hours. They found it very painful
to remain on the ice, and were often obliged to plunge into
the water up to their middle; their seal-skin garments protected them but imperfectly from the damp.

Moreover, all excessive toil in those high latitudes is soon
followed by an overwhelming weariness; for the breath soon
fails, and the strongest are forced to rest at frequent intervals. At last the navigation became free, and the brig was
towed beyond the mass which had so long obstructed her
course.

CHAPTER VI
THE QUAKING OF THE ICE

FOR several days the *Jeune-Hardie* struggled against formidable obstacles. The crew were almost all the time at
work with the saws, and often powder was used to blow up
the enormous blocks of ice which closed the way.

On the 12th of September the sea consisted of one solid
plain, without outlet or passage, surrounding the vessel on
all sides, so that she could neither advance nor retreat. The
temperature remained at an average of sixteen degrees be-

low zero. The winter season had come on, with its sufferings and dangers. The *Jeune-Hardie* was at this time
near the 21st degree of longitude west and the 76th
degree of latitude north, at the entrance of Gaêl-Hamkes
Bay.

Jean Cornbutte made his preliminary preparations for
wintering. He first searched for a creek whose position
would shelter the ship from the wind and breaking up of
the ice. Land, which was probably thirty miles west, could
alone offer him secure shelter, and he resolved to attempt to
reach it.

He set out on the 12th of September, accompanied by
André Vasling, Penellan, and the two sailors Gradlin and
Turquiette. Each man carried provisions for two days, for
it was not likely that their expedition would occupy a longer
time, and they were supplied with skins on which to sleep.

Snow had fallen in great abundance and was not yet
frozen over; and this delayed them seriously. They often
sank to their waists, and could only advance very cautiously,
for fear of falling into crevices. Penellan, who walked in
front, carefully sounded each depression with his iron-
pointed staff.

About five in the evening the fog began to thicken, and
the little band were forced to stop. Penellan looked about
for an iceberg which might shelter them from the wind, and
after refreshing themselves, with regrets that they had no
warm drink, they spread their skins on the snow, wrapped
themselves up, lay close to each other, and soon dropped
asleep from sheer fatigue.

The next morning Jean Cornbutte and his companions
were buried beneath a bed of snow more than a foot deep.
Happily their skins, perfectly impermeable, had preserved
them, and the snow itself had aided in retaining their heat,
which it prevented from escaping.

The captain gave the signal of departure, and about noon
they at last descried the coast, which at first they could
scarcely distinguish. High ledges of ice, cut perpendicularly, rose on the shore; their variegated summits, of all
forms and shapes, reproduced on a large scale the phe-
nomena of crystallization. Myriads of aquatic fowl flew
about at the approach of the party, and the seals, lazily lying
on the ice, plunged hurriedly into the depths.

"I' faith!" said Penellan, "we shall not want for either furs or game!"

"Those animals," returned Cornbutte, "give every evidence of having been already visited by men; for in places totally uninhabited they would not be so wild."

"None but Greenlanders frequent these parts," said André Vasling.

"I see no trace of their passage, however; neither any encampment nor the smallest hut," said Penellan, who had climbed up a high peak. "O captain!" he continued, "come here! I see a point of land which will shelter us splendidly from the northeast wind."

"Come along, boys!" said Jean Cornbutte.

His companions followed him, and they soon rejoined Penellan. The sailor had said what was true. An elevated point of land jutted out like a promontory, and curving towards the coast, formed a little inlet of a mile in width at most. Some moving ice-blocks, broken by this point, floated in the midst, and the sea, sheltered from the colder winds, was not yet entirely frozen over.

This was an excellent spot for wintering, and it only remained to get the ship thither. Jean Cornbutte remarked that the neighboring ice-field was very thick, and it seemed very difficult to cut a canal to bring the brig to its destination. Some other creek, then, must be found; it was in vain that he explored northward. The coast remained steep and abrupt for a long distance, and beyond the point it was directly exposed to the attacks of the east wind. The circumstance disconcerted the captain all the more because André Vasling used strong arguments to show how bad the situation was. Penellan, in his dilemma, found it difficult to convince himself that all was for the best.

But one chance remained—to seek a shelter on the southern side of the coast. This was to return on their path, but hesitation was useless. The little band returned rapidly in the direction of the ship, as their provisions had begun to run short. Jean Cornbutte searched for some practicable passage, or at least some fissure by which a canal might be cut across the ice-fields, all along the route, but in vain.

Towards evening the sailors came to the same place where they had encamped over night. There had been no snow during the day, and they could recognize the imprint of their bodies on the ice. They again disposed themselves to sleep with their furs.

Penellan, much disturbed by the bad success of the expedition, was sleeping restlessly, when, at a waking moment, his attention was attracted by a dull rumbling. He listened attentively, and the rumbling seemed so strange that he nudged Jean Cornbutte with his elbow.

"What is that?" said the latter, whose mind, according to a sailor's habit, was awake as soon as his body.

"Listen, captain."

The noise increased, with perceptible violence.

"It cannot be thunder, in so high a latitude," said Cornbutte, rising.

"I think we have come across some white bears," replied Penellan.

"The devil! We have not seen any yet."

"Sooner or later, we must have expected a visit from them. Let us give them a good reception."

Penellan, armed with a gun, lightly crossed the ledge which sheltered them. The darkness was very dense; he could discover nothing; but a new incident soon showed him that the cause of the noise did not proceed from around them.

Jean Cornbutte rejoined him, and they observed with terror that this rumbling, which awakened their companions, came from beneath them.

A new kind of peril menaced them. To the noise, which resembled peals of thunder, was added a distinct undulating motion of the ice-field. Several of the party lost their balance and fell.

"Attention!" cried Penellan.

"Yes!" someone responded.

"Turquiette! Gradlin! where are you?"

"Here I am!" responded Turquiette, shaking off the snow with which he was covered.

"This way, Vasling," cried Cornbutte to the mate. "And Gradlin?"

"Present, captain."

"But we are lost!" shouted Gradlin, in fright.

"No!" said Penellan. "Perhaps we are saved!"

Hardly had he uttered these words when a frightful cracking noise was heard. The ice-field broke clear through, and the sailors were forced to cling to the block which was quivering just by them. Despite the helmsman's words, they found themselves in a most perilous position, for an ice-quake had occurred. The ice masses had just "weighed anchor," as the sailors say. The movement lasted nearly two minutes, and it was to be feared that the crevice would yawn at the very feet of the unhappy sailors. They anxiously awaited daylight in the midst of continuous shocks, for they could not, without risk of death, move a step, and had to remain stretched out at full length to avoid being engulfed.

As soon as it was daylight a very different aspect presented itself to their eyes. The vast plain, a compact mass the evening before, was now separated in a thousand places, and the waves, raised by some submarine commotion, had broken the thick layer which sheltered them.

The thought of his ship occurred to Cornbutte's mind.

"My poor brig!" he cried. "It must have perished!"

The deepest despair began to overcast the faces of his companions. The loss of the ship inevitably preceded their own deaths.

"Courage, friends," said Penellan. "Reflect that this night's disaster has opened us a path across the ice, which will enable us to bring our ship to the bay for wintering! and, stop! I am not mistaken. There is the *Jeune-Hardie*, a mile nearer to us!"

All hurried forward, and so imprudently, that Turquiette slipped into a fissure, and would have certainly perished, had not Jean Cornbutte seized him by his hood. He got off with a rather cold bath.

The brig was indeed floating two miles away. After infinite trouble, the little band reached her. She was in good condition; but her rudder, which they had neglected to lift, had been broken by the ice.

CHAPTER VII
SETTLING FOR THE WINTER

PENELLAN was once more right; all was for the best, and this ice-quake had opened a practicable channel for the ship to the bay. The sailors had only to make skilful use of the currents to conduct her thither.

On the 19th of September the brig was at last moored in her bay for wintering, two cables' lengths from the shore, securely anchored on a good bottom. The ice began the next day to form around her hull; it soon became strong enough to bear a man's weight, and they could establish a communication with land.

The rigging, as is customary in arctic navigation, remained as it was; the sails were carefully furled on the yards and covered with their casings, and the "crow's-nest" remained in place, as much to enable them to make distant observations as to attract attention to the ship.

The sun now scarcely rose above the horizon. Since the June solstice, the spirals which it had described descended lower and lower; and it would very soon disappear altogether.

The crew hastened to make the necessary preparations. Penellan supervised the whole. The ice was soon thick around the ship, and it was to be feared that its pressure might become dangerous; but Penellan waited until, by reason of the going and coming of the floating ice-masses and their adherence, it had reached a thickness of twenty feet; he then had it cut around the hull, so that it united under the ship, the form of which it assumed; thus enclosed in a mould, the brig had no longer to fear the pressure of the ice, which could make no movement.

The sailors then elevated along the wales to the height of the nettings, a snow wall five or six feet thick, which soon froze as hard as a rock. This envelope did not allow the interior heat to escape outside. A canvas tent, covered with skins and hermetically closed, was stretched over the whole length of the deck, and formed a sort of walk for the sailors.

They also constructed on the ice a storehouse of snow, in which articles which embarrassed the ship were stowed away. The partitions of the cabins were taken down, so as to form a single vast apartment forward, as well as aft. This single room, besides, was more easy to warm, as the ice and damp found fewer corners in which to take refuge. It was also less difficult to ventilate it, by means of canvas funnels which opened without.

Each sailor exerted great energy in these preparations, and about the 25th of September they were completed. André Vasling had not shown himself the least active in

this task. He devoted himself with especial zeal to the
young girl's comfort, and if she, absorbed in thoughts of her
poor Louis, did not perceive this, Jean Cornbutte did not
fail soon to remark it. He spoke of it to Penellan; he
recalled several incidents which completely enlightened him
regarding his mate's intentions; André Vasling loved Marie,
and reckoned on asking her uncle for her hand, as soon as
it was proved beyond doubt that the castaways were irrevoc-
ably lost; they would return then to Dunkirk, and André
Vasling would be well satisfied to wed a rich and pretty girl,
who would then be the sole heiress of Jean Cornbutte.

But André, in his impatience, was often imprudent. He
had several times declared that the search for the castaways
was useless, when some new trace contradicted him, and
enabled Penellan to exult over him. The mate, therefore,
cordially detested the helmsman, who returned his dislike
heartily. Penellan only feared that André might sow seeds
of dissension among the crew, and persuaded Jean Cornbutte
to answer him evasively on the first occasion.

The sky, always gloomy, filled the soul with sadness. A
thick snow, lashed by violent winds, added to the horrors
of their situation. The sun would soon altogether disappear. Had the clouds not gathered in masses above their
heads, they might have enjoyed the moonlight, which was
about to become really their sun during the long polar night;
but, with the west winds, the snow did not cease to fall.
Every morning it was necessary to clear off the sides of the
ship, and to cut a new stairway in the ice to enable them to
reach the ice-field. Penellan had a hole cut in the ice, not
far from the ship. Every day the new crust which formed
over its top was broken, and the water which was drawn
thence, from a certain depth, was less cold than that at the
surface.

All these preparations occupied about three weeks. It
was then time to go forward with the search. The ship
was imprisoned for six or seven months, and only the next
thaw could open a new route across the ice. It was wise,
then, to profit by this delay, and extend their explorations
northward.

CHAPTER VIII
PLAN OF THE EXPLORATIONS

On the 9th of October, Jean Cornbutte held a council to settle the plan of his operations, to which, that there might be union, zeal, and courage on the part of everyone, he admitted the whole crew. Map in hand, he clearly explained their situation.

The eastern coast of Greenland advances perpendicularly northward. The discoveries of the navigators have given the exact boundaries of those parts. In the extent of five hundred leagues, which separates Greenland from Spitzbergen, no land has been found. An island (Shannon Island) lay a hundred miles north of Gaël-Hamkes Bay, where the *Jeune-Hardie* was wintering.

If the Norwegian schooner, as was most probable, had been driven in this direction, supposing that she could not reach Shannon Island, it was here that Louis Cornbutte and his comrades must have sought for a winter asylum.

This opinion prevailed, despite André Vasling's opposition; and it was decided to direct the explorations on the side towards Shannon Island. If Louis Cornbutte and his comrades were still in existence, it was not probable that they would be able to resist the severities of the arctic winter. They must therefore be saved beforehand, or all hope would be lost. André Vasling knew all this better than anyone. He therefore resolved to put every possible obstacle in the way of the expedition.

The preparations for the journey were completed about the 20th of October. It remained to select the men who should compose the party. The young girl could not be deprived of the protection of Jean Cornbutte or of Penellan; neither of these could, on the other hand, be spared from the expedition.

The question, then, was whether Marie could bear the fatigues of such a journey. She had already passed through rough experiences without seeming to suffer from them, for she was a sailor's daughter, used from infancy to the fatigues of the sea, and even Penellan was not dismayed to see her struggling in the midst of this severe climate, against the dangers of the polar seas.

It was decided, therefore, after a long discussion, that she should go with them, and that a place should be reserved

for her, at need, on the sledge, on which a little wooden
hut was constructed, closed in hermetically. As for Marie,
she was delighted, for she dreaded to be left alone without
her two protectors.

The expedition was thus formed: Marie, Jean Cornbutte,
Penellan, André Vasling, Aupic, and Fidèle Misonne were
to go. Alaine Turquiette remained in charge of the brig,
and Gervique and Gradlin stayed behind with him. New
provisions of all kinds were carried; for Jean Cornbutte,
in order to carry the exploration as far as possible, had
resolved to establish depots along the route, at each seven
or eight days' march. When the sledge was ready it was
at once fitted up, and covered with a skin tent. The whole
weighed some seven hundred pounds, which a pack of five
dogs might easily carry over the ice.

On the 22nd of October, as the captain had foretold, a
sudden change took place in the temperature. The sky
cleared, the stars emitted an extraordinary light, and the
moon shone above the horizon, no longer to leave the
heavens for a fortnight. The thermometer descended to
twenty-five degrees below zero. The departure was fixed
for the following day.

CHAPTER IX
THE HOUSE OF SNOW

On the 23rd of October, at eleven in the morning, in a fine
moonlight, the caravan set out. Jean Cornbutte followed
the coast, and ascended northward. The steps of the travelers made no impression on the hard ice. Jean was forced to
guide himself by points which he selected at a distance;
sometimes he fixed upon a hill bristling with peaks; sometimes on a vast iceberg which pressure had raised above the
plain.

At the first halt, after going fifteen miles, Penellan prepared to encamp. The tent was erected against an ice-block.
Marie had not suffered seriously with the extreme cold, for
luckily the breeze had subsided, and was much more bear-
able; but the young girl had several times been obliged to
descend from her sledge to avert numbness from imped-
ing the circulation of her blood. Otherwise, her little hut,

hung with skins, afforded her all the comfort possible under the circumstances.

When night, or rather sleeping-time, came, the little hut was carried under the tent, where it served as a bed-room for Marie. The evening repast was composed of fresh meat, pemmican, and hot tea. Jean Cornbutte, to avert danger of the scurvy, distributed to each of the party a few drops of lemon-juice. Then all slept under God's protection.

But the sailors soon began to suffer one discomfort—that of being dazzled. Ophthalmia betrayed itself in Aupic and Misonne. The moon's light, striking on these vast white plains, burnt the eyesight, and gave the eyes insupportable pain. There was thus produced a very singlar effect of refraction. As they walked, when they thought they were about to put foot on a hillock, they stepped down lower, which often occasioned falls, happily so little serious that Penellan made them occasions for bantering. Still, he told them never to take a step without sounding the ground with the ferruled staff with which each was equipped.

About the 1st of November, ten days after they had set out, the caravan had gone fifty leagues to the northward. Weariness pressed heavily on all. Jean Cornbutte was painfully dazzled and his sight sensibly changed. Aupic and Misonne had to feel their way: for their eyes, rimmed with red, seemed burnt by the white reflection. Marie had been preserved from this misfortune by remaining within her hut, to which she confined herself as much as possible. Penellan, sustained by an indomitable courage, resisted all fatigue. But it was André Vasling who bore himself best, and upon whom the cold and dazzling seemed to produce no effect. His iron frame was equal to every hardship; and he was secretly pleased to see the most robust of his companions becoming discouraged, and already foresaw the moment when they would be forced to retreat to the ship again.

On the 1st of November it became absolutely necessary to halt for a day or two. As soon as the place for the encampment had been selected, they proceeded to arrange it. It was determined to erect a house of snow, which should be supported against one of the rocks of the promontory. Misonne at once marked out the foundations, which measured fifteen feet long by five wide. Penellan,

Aupic, and Misonne, by aid of their knives, cut out great blocks of ice, which they carried to the chosen spot and set up, as masons would have built stone walls. The sides of the foundation were soon raised to a height and thickness of about five feet; for the materials were abundant, and the structure was intended to be sufficiently solid to last several days. The four walls were completed in eight hours; an opening had been left on the southern side, and the canvas of the tent, placed on these four walls, fell over the opening and sheltered it. It only remained to cover the whole with large blocks, to form the roof of this temporary structure.

After three more hours of hard work, the house was done; and they all went into it, overcome with weariness and discouragement. Jean Cornbutte suffered so much that he could not walk, and André Vasling so skillfully aggravated his gloomy feelings, that he forced from him a promise not to pursue his search farther in those frightful solitudes. Penellan did not know which saint to invoke. He thought it unworthy and craven to give up the search for reasons which had little weight, and tried to upset them; but in vain.

Meanwhile, though it had been decided to return, rest had become so necessary that for three days no preparations for departure were made. On the 4th of November, Jean Cornbutte began to bury on a point of the coast the provisions for which there was no use. A stake indicated the place of the deposit, in the improbable event that new explorations should be made in that direction. Every day since they had set out similar deposits had been made, so that they were assured of ample sustenance on the return, without the trouble of carrying them on the sledge.

The departure was fixed for ten in the morning, on the 5th. The most profound sadness filled the little band. Marie with difficulty restrained her tears, when she saw her uncle so completely discouraged. So many useless sufferings! so much labor lost! Penellan himself became ferocious in his ill-humor; he consigned everybody to the nether regions, and did not cease to wax angry at the weakness and cowardice of his comrades, who were more timid and tired, he said, than Marie, who would have gone to the end of the world without complaint

André Vasling could not disguise the pleasure which this decision gave him. He showed himself more attentive than ever to the young girl, to whom he even held out hopes that a new search should be made when the winter was over; knowing well that it would then be too late!

CHAPTER X
BURIED ALIVE

THE evening before the departure, just as they were about to take supper, Penellan was breaking up some empty casks for firewood, when he was suddenly suffocated by a thick smoke. At the same instant the snow-house was shaken as if by an earthquake. The party uttered a cry of terror, and Penellan hurried outside.

It was entirely dark. A frightful tempest—for it was not a thaw—was raging, whirlwinds of snow careered around, and it was so exceedinly cold that the helmsman felt his hands rapidly freezing. He was obliged to go in again, after rubbing himself violently with snow.

"It is a tempest," said he. "May heaven grant that our house may withstand it, for, if the storm should destroy it, we should be lost!"

At the same time with the gusts of wind a noise was heard beneath the frozen soil; icebergs, broken from the promontory, dashed away noisily, and fell upon one another; the wind blew with such violence that it seemed sometimes as if the whole house moved from its foundation; phosphorescent lights, inexplicable in that latitude, flashed across the whirlwinds of the snow.

"Marie! Marie!" cried Penellan, seizing the girl's hands.

"We are in a bad case!" said Misonne.

"I know not if we shall escape," replied Aupic.

"Let us quit this snow-house!" said André Vasling.

"Impossible!" returned Penellan. "The cold outside is terrible; perhaps we can bear it by staying here."

"Give me the thermometer," demanded Vasling.

Aupic handed it to him. It showed ten degrees below zero inside the house, though the fire was lighted. Vasling raised the canvas which covered the opening, and pushed it aside hastily; for he would have been lacerated by the fall of ice which the wind hurled around, and which fell in a perfect hail-storm.

"Well, Vasling," said Penellan, "will you go out, then? You see that we are more safe here."

"Yes," said Jean Cornbutte; "and we must use every effort to strengthen the house in the interior."

"But a still more terrible danger menaces us," said Vasling.

"What?" asked Jean.

"The wind is breaking the ice against which we are propped, just as it has that of the promontory, and we shall be either driven out or buried!"

"That seems doubtful," said Penellan, "for it is freezing hard enough to ice over all liquid surfaces. Let us see what the temperature is."

He raised the canvas so as to pass out his arm, and with difficulty found the thermometer again, in the midst of the snow; but he at last succeeded in seizing it, and, holding the lamp to it, said, "Thirty-two degrees below zero! It is the coldest we have seen here yet!"

"Ten degrees more," said Vasling, "and the mercury will freeze!"

A mournful silence followed this remark.

About eight in the morning Penellan essayed a second time to go out to judge of their situation. It was necessary to give an escape to the smoke, which the wind had several timse repelled into the hut. The sailor wrapped his cloak tightly about him, made sure of his hood by fastening it to his head with a handkerchief, and then raised the canvas.

The opening was entirely obstructed by a resisting snow. Penellan took his staff, and succeeded in plunging it into the compact mass; but terror froze his blood when he perceived that the end of the staff was not free, and was checked by a hard body!

"Cornbutte," said he to the captain, who had come up to him, "we are buried under this snow!"

"What say you?" cried Jean Cornbutte.

"I say that the snow is massed and frozen around us and over us, and that we are buried alive!"

"Let us make an effort to clear the snow away," replied the captain.

The two friends buttressed themselves against the obstacle which obstructed the opening, but they could not move it. The snow formed an iceberg more than five feet thick, and had become literally a part of the house. Jean could not suppress a cry, which awoke Misonne and Vasling. An oath burst from the latter, whose features contracted. At this moment the smoke, thicker than ever, poured into the house, for it could not find an issue.

"Malediction!" cried Misonne. "The pipe of the stove is sealed up by the ice!"

Penellan resumed his staff, and took down the pipe, after throwing snow on the embers to extinguish them, which produced such a smoke that the light of the lamp could scarcely be seen; then he tried with his staff to clear out the orifice, but he only encountered a rock of ice! A frightful end, preceded by a terrible agony, seemed to be their doom! The smoke, penetrating the throats of the unfortunate party, caused an insufferable pain, and air would soon fail them altogether.

Marie here rose, and her presence, which inspired Cornbutte with despair, imparted some courage to Penellan. He said to himself that it could not be that the poor girl was destined to so horrible a death.

"Ah!" said she, "you have made too much fire. The room is full of smoke!"

"Yes, yes," stammered Penellan.

"It is evident," resumed Marie, " for it is not cold, and it is long since we have felt too much heat."

No one dared to tell her the truth.

"See, Marie," said Penellan bluntly, "help us get breakfast ready. It is too cold to go out. Here is the chafing-dish, the spirit, and the coffee. Come, you others, a little pemmican first, as this wretched storm forbids us from hunting."

These words stirred up his comrades.

"Let us first eat," added Penellan, "and then we shall see about getting off."

Penellan set the example and devoured his share of the breakfast. His comrades imitated him, and then drank a cup of boiling coffee, which somewhat restored their spirits. Then Jean Cornbutte decided energetically that they should at once set about devising means of safety.

André Vasling now said, "If the storm is still raging, which is probable, we must be buried ten feet under the ice, for we can hear no noise outside."

Penellan looked at Marie, who now understood the truth, and did not tremble. The helmsman first heated, by the flame of the spirit, the iron point of his staff, and successfully introduced it into the four walls of ice, but he could find no issue in either. Cornbutte then resolved to cut out an opening in the door itself. The ice was so hard that it was difficult for the knives to make the least impression on it. The pieces which were cut off soon encumbered the hut. After working hard for two hours, they had only hollowed out a space three feet deep.

Some more rapid method, and one which was less likely to demolish the house, must be thought of; for the farther they advanced the more violent became the effort to break off the compact ice. It occurred to Penellan to make use of the chafing-dish to melt the ice in the direction they wanted. It was a hazardous method, for, if their imprisonment lasted long, the spirit, of which they had but little, would be wanting when needed to prepare the meals. Nevertheless, the idea was welcomed on all hands, and was put in execution. They first cut a hole three feet deep by one in diameter, to receive the water which would result from the melting of the ice; and it was well that they took this precaution, for the water soon dripped under the action of the flames, which Penellan moved about under the mass of ice. The opening widened little by little, but this kind of work could not be continued long, for the water covering their clothes, penetrated to their bodies here and there. Penellan was obliged to pause in a quarter of an hour, and to withdraw the chafing-dish in order to dry himself. Misonne then took his place, and worked sturdily at the task.

In two hours, though the opening was five feet deep, the points of the staffs could not yet find an issue through the ice.

"It is not possible," said Jean Cornbutte, "that snow could have fallen in such abundance. It must have been gathered on this point by the wind. Perhaps we had better think of escaping in some other direction."

"I don't know," replied Penellan; "but if it were only

for the sake of not discouraging our comrades, we ought to continue to pierce the wall where we have begun. We must find an issue ere long."

" Will not the spirit fail us? " asked the captain.

" I hope not. But let us, if necessary, dispense with coffee and hot drinks. Besides, that is not what most alarms me."

" What is it, then, Penellan? "

" Our lamp is going out, for want of oil, and we are fast exhausting our provisions."

The time for rest had come, and when Penellan had added one more foot to the opening, he lay down beside his comrades.

CHAPTER XI
A CLOUD OF SMOKE

THE next day, when the sailors awoke, they were surrounded by complete darkness. The lamp had gone out. Jean Cornbutte roused Penellan to ask him for the tinderbox, which was passed to him. Penellan rose to light the fire, but in getting up, his head struck against the ice ceiling. He was horrified, for on the evening before he could still stand upright. The chafing-dish being lighted up by the dim rays of the spirit, he perceived that the ceiling was a foot lower than before.

Penellan resumed work with desperation.

Marie, by the light which the chafing-dish cast upon Penellan's face, saw that despair and determination were struggling in his rough features for the mastery. She went to him, took his hands, and tenderly pressed them.

" She cannot, must not die thus ! " he cried.

He took his chafing-dish, and once more attcked the narrow opening. He plunged in his staff, and felt no resistance. Had he reached the soft layers of the snow? He drew out his staff, and a bright ray penetrated to the house of ice !

" Here, my friends ! " he shouted.

He pushed back the snow with his hands and feet. With the rays of light, a violent cold entered the cabin and seized upon everything moist, to freeze it in an instant. Penellan enlarged the opening with his cutlass, and at last was able to breathe the free air. He fell on his knees to thank God, and was soon joined by Marie and his comrades.

A magnificent moon lit up the sky, but the cold was so extreme that they could not bear it. They re-entered their retreat; but Penellan first looked about him. The promontory was no longer there, and the hut was now in the midst of a vast plain of ice. Penellan thought he would go to the sledge, where the provisions were. The sledge had disappeared!

The cold forced him to return. He said nothing to his companions. It was necessary, before all, to dry their clothing, which was done with the chafing-dish. The thermometer, held for an instant in the air, descended to thirty degrees below zero.

An hour after, Vasling and Penellan resolved to venture outside. They wrapped themselves up in their still wet garments, and went out by the opening, the sides of which had become as hard as a rock.

"We have been driven towards the northeast," said Vasling, reckoning by the stars.

"That would not be bad," said Penellan, "if our sledge had come with us."

"Is not the sledge there?" cried Vasling. "Then we are lost!"

"Let us look for it," replied Penellan.

They went around the hut, which formed a block more than fifteen feet high. An immense quantity of snow had fallen during the whole of the storm, and the wind had massed it against the only elevation which the plain presented. The entire block had been driven by the wind, in the midst of the broken icebergs, more than twenty-five miles to the northeast, and the prisoners had suffered the same fate as their floating prison. The sledge, supported by another iceberg, had been turned another way, for no trace of it was to be seen, and the dogs must have perished amid the frightful tempest.

André Vasling and Penellan felt despair taking possession of them. They did not dare to return to their companions. They did not dare to announce this fatal news to their comrades in misfortune. They climbed upon the block of ice in which the hut was hollowed, and could perceive nothing but the white immensity which encompassed them on all sides. Already the cold was beginning to stiffen their limbs, and the damp of their garments was being transformed into icicles which hung about them.

Just as Penellan was about to descend, he looked towards André. He saw him suddenly gaze in one direction, then shudder and turn pale.

"What is the matter, Vasling?" he asked.

"Nothing," replied the other. "Let us go down and urge the captain to leave these parts, where we ought never to have come, at once!"

Instead of obeying, Penellan ascended again, and looked in the direction which had drawn the mate's attention. A very different effect was produced on him, for he uttered a shout of joy, and cried, "Blessed be God!"

A light smoke was rising in the northeast. There was no possibility of deception. It indicated the presence of human beings. Penellan's cries of joy reached the rest below, and all were able to convince themselves with their eyes that he was not mistaken.

Without thinking of their want of provisions or the severity of the temperature, wrapped in their hoods, they were all soon advancing towards the spot whence the smoke arose in the northeast. This was evidently five or six miles off, and it was very difficult to take exactly the right direction. The smoke now disappeared, and no elevation served as a guiding mark, for the ice-plain was one united level. It was important, nevertheless, not to diverge from a straight line.

"Since we cannot guide ourselves by distant objects," said Jean Cornbutte, "we must use this method. Penellan will go ahead, Vasling twenty steps behind him, and I twenty steps behind Vasling. I can then judge whether or not Penellan diverges from the straight line."

They had gone on thus for half an hour, when Penellan suddenly stopped and listened. The party hurried up to him. "Did you hear nothing?" he asked.

"Nothing!" replied Misonne.

"It is strange," said Penellan. "It seemed to me I heard cries off to one side from this direction."

"Cries?" replied Marie. "Perhaps we are near our destination, then."

"That is no reason," said André Vasling. "In these

high latitudes and cold regions sounds may be heard to a great distance."

"However that may be," replied Jean Cornbutte, "let us go forward, or we shall be frozen."

"No!" cried Penellan. "Listen!"

Some feeble sounds—quite perceptible, however—were heard. They seemed to be cries of distress. They were twice repeated. They seemed like cries for help. Then all became silent again.

"I was not mistaken," said Penellan. "Forward!"

He began to run in the direction whence the cries had proceeded. He went thus two miles, when, to his utter stupefaction, he saw a man lying on the ice. He went up to him, raised him, and lifted his arms to heaven in despair.

André Vasling, who was following close behind with the rest of the sailors, ran up and cried, "It is one of the castaways! It is our sailor Courtois!"

"He is dead!" replied Penellan. "Frozen to death!"

Jean Cornbutte and Marie came up beside the corpse, which was already stiffened by the ice. Despair was written on every face. The dead man was one of the comrades of Louis Cornbutte!

"Forward!" cried Penellan.

They went on for half an hour in perfect silence, and perceived an elevation which seemed to be land.

"It is Shannon Island," said Jean Cornbutte.

A mile farther on they saw smoke escaping from a snow-hut, closed by a wooden door. They shouted. Two men rushed out of the hut, and Penellan recognized one of them as Pierre Nouquet. "Pierre!" he cried.

Pierre stood still as if stunned, and unconscious of what was going on around him. André Vasling looked at Pierre Nouquet's companion with anxiety mingled with a cruel joy, for it was not Louis Cornbutte.

"Pierre! it is I" cried Penellan. "We are your friends!"

Pierre Nouquet recovered his senses, and fell into his old comrade's arms.

"And my son—and Louis!" cried Jean Cornbutte, in an accent of the most profound despair.

CHAPTER XII
THE RETURN TO THE SHIP

At this moment a man, almost dead, dragged himself out of the hut and along the ice. It was Louis Cornbutte.

" My son! "

" My beloved! "

These two cries were uttered at the same time, and Louis Cornbutte fell fainting into the arms of his father and Marie, who drew him towards the hut, where their tender care soon revived him.

" My father! Marie! " cried Louis; " I shall not die without having seen you! "

" You will not die! " replied Penellan, " for all your friends are near you."

André Vasling must have hated Louis Cornbutte bitterly not to extend his hand to him, but he did not.

Pierre Nouquet was wild with joy. He embraced everybody; then he threw some wood into the stove, and soon a comfortable temperature was felt in the cabin.

There were two men there whom neither Jean Cornbutte nor Penellan recognized.

They were Jocki and Herming, the only two sailors of the crew of the Norwegian schooner who were left.

" My friends, we are saved! " said Louis. " My father! Marie! You have exposed yourselves to so many perils! "

" We do not regret it, my Louis," replied the father. " Your brig, the *Jeune-Hardie,* is securely anchored in the ice sixty leagues from here. We will rejoin her all together."

" When Courtois comes back he'll be mightily pleased," said Pierre Nouquet.

A mournful silence followed this, and Penellan apprised Pierre and Louis of their comrade's death by cold.

" My friends," said Penellan, " we will wait here until the cold decreases. Have you provisions and wood? "

" Yes; and we will burn what is left of the *Froöern."*

The *Froöern* had indeed been driven to a place forty miles from where Louis Cornbutte had taken up his winter quarters. There she was broken up by the icebergs floated by the thaw, and the castaways were carried, with a part of the débris of their cabin, on the southern shores of Shannon Island.

They were then five in number—Louis Cornbutte, Courtois, Pierre Nouquet, Jocki, and Herming. As for the rest of the Norwegian crew, they had been submerged with the long-boat at the moment of the wreck.

When Louis Cornbutte, shut in among the ice, realized what must happen, he took every precaution for passing the winter. He was an energetic man, very active and courageous; but, despite his firmness, he had been subdued by this horrible climate, and when his father found him he had given up all hope of life. He had not only had to contend with the elements, but with the ugly temper of the two Norwegian sailors, who owed him their existence. They were like savages, almost inaccessible to the most natural emotions. When Louis had the opportunity to talk to Penellan, he advised him to watch them carefully. In return, Penellan told him of André Vasling's conduct. Louis could not believe it, but Penellan convinced him that after his disappearance Vasling had always acted so as to secure Marie's hand.

The whole day was employed in rest and the pleasures of reunion. Misonne and Pierre Nouquet killed some sea-birds near the hut, whence it was not prudent to stray far. These fresh provisions and the replenished fire raised the spirits of the weakest. Louis Cornbutte got visibly better. It was the first moment of happiness these brave people had experienced. They celebrated it with enthusiasm in this wretched hut, six hundred leagues from the North Sea, in a temperature of thirty degrees below zero!

This temperature lasted till the end of the moon, and it was not until about the 17th of November, a week after their meeting, that Jean Cornbutte and his party could think of setting out. They only had the light of the stars to guide them; but the cold was less extreme, and even some snow fell.

Before quitting this place a grave was dug for poor Courtois. It was a sad ceremony, which deeply affected his comrades. He was the first of them who would not again see his native land.

Misonne had constructed, with the planks of the cabin, a sort of sledge for carrying the provisions, and the sailors drew it by turns. Jean Cornbutte led the expedition by the ways already traversed. Camps were established with great promptness when the times for repose came. Jean Cornbutte hoped to find his deposits of provisions again, as they had become well-nigh indispensable by the addition of four persons to the party. He was therefore very careful not to diverge from the route by which he had come.

By good fortune he recovered his sledge, which had stranded near the promontory where they had all run so many dangers. The dogs, after eating their straps to satisfy their hunger, had attacked the provisions in the sledge. These had sustained them, and they served to guide the party to the sledge, where there was a considerable quantity of provisions left. The little band resumed its march towards the bay. The dogs were harnessed to the sleigh, and no event of interest attended the return.

It was observed that Aupic, André Vasling, and the Norwegians kept aloof, and did not mingle with the others; but, unbeknown to themselves, they were narrowly watched. This germ of dissension more than once aroused the fears of Louis Cornbutte and Penellan.

About the 7th of December, twenty days after the discovery of the castaways, they perceived the bay where the *Jeune-Hardie* was lying. What was their astonishment to see the brig perched four yards in the air on blocks of ice! They hurried forward, much alarmed for their companions, and were received with joyous cries by Gervique, Turquiette, and Gradlin. All of them were in good health, though they too had been subjected to formidable dangers.

The tempest had made itself felt throughout the polar sea. The ice had been broken and displaced, crushed one piece against another, and had seized the bed on which the ship rested. Though its specific weight tended to carry it under water, the ice had acquired an incalculable force, and the brig had been suddenly raised up out of the sea.

The first moments were given up to the happiness inspired by the safe return. The exploring party were rejoiced to find everything in good condition, which assured them a supportable though it might be a rough winter. The ship had not been shaken by her sudden elevation, and was perfectly tight. When the season of thawing came, they would only have to slide her down an inclined plane, to launch her, in a word, in the once more open sea.

But a bad piece of news spread gloom on the faces of
Jean Cornbutte and his comrades. During the terrible
gale the snow storehouse on the coast had been quite de-
molished; the provisions which it contained were scattered,
and it had not been possible to save a morsel of them.
When Jean and Louis Cornbutte learned this, they visited
the hold and steward's room, to ascertain the quantity of
provisions which still remained.

The thaw would not come until May, and the brig could
not leave the bay before that period. They had therefore
five winter months before them to pass amid the ice, during
which fourteen persons were to be fed. Having made his
calculations, Jean Cornbutte found that he would at most
be able to keep them alive till the time for departure, by
putting each and all on half rations. Hunting for game
became compulsory in order to procure food in larger quantity.

For fear that they might again run short of provisions, it
was decided to deposit them no longer in the ground. All
of them were kept on board, and beds were disposed for
the newcomers in the common lodging. Turquiette, Gervique, and Gradlin, during the absence of the others, had
hollowed out a flight of steps in the ice, which enabled them
easily to reach the ship's deck.

CHAPTER XIII

THE TWO RIVALS

ANDRE VASLING had been cultivating the good-will of
the two Norwegian sailors. Aupic also made one of their
band, and held himself apart, with loud disapproval of all
the new measures taken; but Louis Cornbutte, to whom his
father had transferred the command of the ship, and who
had become once more master on board, would listen to no
objections from that quarter, and in spite of Marie's advice
to act gently, made it known that he intended to be obeyed
on all points.

Nevertheless, the two Norwegians succeeded two days
after, in getting possession of a box of salt meat. Louis
ordered them to return it to him on the spot, but Aupic

took their part, and André Vasling declared that the precautions about food could not be any longer enforced.

It was useless to attempt to show these men that these measures were for the common interest, for they knew it well, and only sought a pretext to revolt.

Penellan advanced towards the Norwegians, who drew their cutlasses; but, aided by Misonne and Turquiette, he succeeded in snatching the weapons from their hands, and gained possession of the salt meat. André Vasling and Aupic, seeing that matters were going against them, did not interfere. Louis Cornbutte, however, took the mate aside, and said to him:

"André Vasling, you are a wretch! I know your whole conduct, and I know what you are aiming at, but as the safety of the whole crew is confided to me, if any man of you thinks of conspiring to destroy them, I will stab him with my own hand!"

"Louis Cornbutte," replied the mate, "it is allowable for you to act the master; but remember that absolute obedience does not exist here, and that here the strongest alone makes the law."

Marie had never trembled before the dangers of the polar seas; but she was terrified by this hatred, of which she was the cause, and the captain's vigor hardly reassured her.

Despite this declaration of war, the meals were partaken of in common and at the same hours. Hunting furnished some ptarmigans and white hares; but this resource would soon fail them, with the approach of the terrible cold weather. This began at the solstice, on the 22d of December, on which day the thermometer fell to thirty-five degrees below zero. The men experienced pain in their ears, noses, and the extremities of their bodies. They were seized with a mortal torpor combined with headache, and their breathing became more and more difficult.

In this state they had no longer any courage to go hunting or to take any exercise. They remained crouched around the stove, which gave them but a meager heat; and when they went away from it, they perceived that their blood suddenly cooled.

Jean Cornbutte's health was seriously impaired, and he could no longer quit his lodging. Symptoms of scurvy manifested themselves in him, and his legs were soon covered with white spots. Marie was well, however, and occupied herself tending the sick ones with the zeal of a sister of charity. The honest fellows blessed her from the bottom of their hearts.

The 1st of January was one of the gloomiest of these winter days. The wind was violent, and the cold insupportable. They could not go out, except at the risk of being frozen. The most courageous were fain to limit themselves to walking on deck, sheltered by the tent. Jean Cornbutte, Gervique, and Gradlin did not leave their beds. The two Norwegians, Aupic, and André Vasling, whose health was good, cast ferocious looks at their companions, whom they saw wasting away.

Louis Cornbutte led Penellan on deck, and asked him how much firing was left.

"The coal was exhausted long ago," replied Penellan, "and we are about to burn our last pieces of wood."

"If we are not able to keep off this cold, we are lost," said Louis.

"There still remains a way—" said Penellan, "to burn what we can of the brig, from the barricading to the water-line; and we can even, if need be, demolish her entirely, and rebuild a smaller craft."

"That is an extreme means," replied Louis, "which it will be full time to employ when our men are well. For," he added in a low voice, "our force is diminishing, and that of our enemies seems to be increasing. That is extraordinary."

"It is true," said Penellan; "and unless we took the precaution to watch night and day, I know not what would happen to us."

"Let us take our hatchets," returned Louis, "and make our harvest of wood."

Despite the cold, they mounted on the forward barricading, and cut off all the wood which was not indispensably necessary to the ship; then they returned with this new provision. The fire was started afresh, and a man remained on guard to prevent it from going out.

Meanwhile Louis Cornbutte and his friends were soon tired out. They could not confide any detail of the life in common to their enemies. Charged with all the domestic cares, their powers were soon exhausted. The scurvy betrayed itself in Jean Cornbutte, who suffered intolerable pain. Gervique and Gradlin showed symptoms of the same disease. Had it not been for the lemon-juice, with which they were abundantly furnished, they would have speedily succumbed to their sufferings. This remedy was not spared in relieving them.

But one day, the 15th of January, when Louis Cornbutte was going down into the steward's room to get some lemons, he was stupefied to find that the barrels in which they were kept had disappeared. He hurried up and told Penellan of this misfortune. A theft had been committed, and it was easy to recognize its authors. Louis Cornbutte then understood why the health of his enemies continued so good! His friends were no longer strong enough to take the lemons away from them, though his life and that of his comrades depended on the fruit; and he now sank, for the first time, into a gloomy state of despair.

CHAPTER XIV
DISTRESS

ON the 20th of January most of the crew had not the strength to leave their beds. Each, independently of his woolen coverings, had a buffalo-skin to protect him against the cold; but as soon as he put his arms outside the clothes, he felt a severe pain which obliged him quickly to cover them again.

Meanwhile, Louis having lit the stove fire, Penellan, Misonne, and André Vasling left their beds and crouched around it. Penellan prepared some boiling coffe, which gave them some strength, as well as Marie, who joined them in partaking of it.

Louis Cornbutte approached his father's bedside; the old man was almost motionless, and his limbs were helpless from disease. He muttered some disconnected words, which carried grief to his son's heart.

"Louis," said he, "I am dying! I suffer! Save me!"

Louis took a decisive resolution. He went up to the mate, and, controlling himself with difficulty, said: "Do you know where the lemons are, Vasling?"

"In the steward's room, I suppose," returned the mate, without stirring.

"You know very well they are not, as you have stolen them!"

"You are master, Louis Cornbutte, and may say and do anything."

"For pity's sake, André Vasling, my father is dying! You can save him,—answer!"

"I have nothing to answer," replied André Vasling.

"Wretch!" cried Penellan, throwing himself, cutlass in hand, on the mate.

"Help, friends!" shouted Vasling, retreating.

'Aupic and the two Norwegian sailors jumped from their beds and placed themselves behind him. Turquiette, Penellan, and Louis prepared to defend themselves. Pierre Nouquet and Gradlin, though suffering much, rose to second them.

"You are still too strong for us," said Vasling. "We do not wish to fight on an uncertainty."

The sailors were so weak that they dared not attack the four rebels, for, had they failed, they would have been lost. "André Vasling!" said Louis, in a gloomy tone, "if my father dies, you will have murdered him; and I will kill you like a dog!"

Vasling and his confederates retired to the other end of the cabin, and did not reply.

It was then necessary to renew the supply of wood, and, in spite of the cold, Louis went on deck and began to cut away a part of the barricading, but was obliged to retreat in a quarter of an hour, for he was in danger of falling, overcome by the freezing air. As he passed, he cast a glance at the thermometer left outside, and saw that the mercury was frozen. The cold, then, exceeded forty-two degrees below zero. The weather was dry, and the wind blew from the north.

On the 26th the wind changed to the northeast, and the thermometer outside stood at thirty-five degrees. Jean Cornbutte was in agony, and his son had searched in vain for some remedy with which to relieve his pain. On this day, however, throwing himself suddenly on Vasling, he managed to snatch a lemon from him which he was about to suck. Vasling made no attempt to recover it. He seemed

A third bear was directing his way towards the ship's prow.
Vasling paid no attention to him, but, followed by Herming,
went to the aid of Jocki; but Jocki, seized by the beast's
paws, was crushed, and when the bear fell under the shots
of the other two men, he held a corpse in his shaggy arms.

"We are only two, now," said Vasling, with gloomy fero-
city, "but if we yield, it will not be without vengeance!"

Herming reloaded his pistol without replying. Before
all, the third bear must be got rid of. Vasling looked forward,
but did not see him. On raising his eyes, he perceived him
erect on the barricading, clinging to the ratlines and trying
to reach Louis. Vasling let his gun fall, which he had
aimed at the animal, while a fierce joy glittered in his eyes.
"Ah," he cried to the bear, "you owe me that vengeance!"

Louis took refuge in the top of the mast. The bear
kept mounting, and was not more than six feet from Louis,
when he raised his gun and pointed it at the animal's heart.

Vasling raised his weapon to shoot Louis if the bear fell.

Louis fired, but the bear did not appear to be hit, for he
leaped with a bound towards the top. The whole mast
shook.

Vasling uttered a shout of exultation.

"Herming," he cried, "go and find Marie! Go and find
my betrothed!"

Herming descended the cabin stairs.

Meanwhile the furious beast had thrown himself upon
Louis, who was trying to shelter himself on the other side
of the mast; but at the moment that his enormous paw
was raised to break his head, Louis, seizing one of the
backstays, let himself slip down to the deck, not without
danger, for a ball hissed by his ear when he was half-way
down. Vasling had shot at him, and missed him. The
two adversaries now confronted each other, cutlass in hand.

The combat was about to become decisive. To glut his
vengeance, and to have the young girl witness her lover's
death, Vasling had deprived himself of Herming's aid. He
could now reckon only on himself.

Louis and Vasling seized each other by the collar, and
held each other with iron grip. One of them must fall.
They struck each other violently. The blows were only
half parried, for blood soon flowed from both. Vasling
tried to clasp his adversary about the neck with his arm,

to bring him to the ground. Louis, knowing that he who fell was lost, prevented him, and succeeded in grasping his two arms; but in doing this he let fall his cutlass.

Pietous cries now assailed his ears; it was Marie's voice. Herming was trying to drag her up. Louis was seized with a desperate rage. He stiffened himself to bend Vasling's loins; but at this moment the combatants felt themselves seized in a powerful embrace. The bear, having descended from the mast, had fallen upon the two men. Vasling was pressed against the animal's body. Louis felt his claws entering his flesh. The bear was strangling both of them.

" Help! help! Herming! " cried the mate.

" Help! Penellan! " cried Louis.

Steps were heard on the stairs. Penellan appeared, loaded his pistol, and discharged it in the bear's ear; he roared; the pain made him relax his paws for a moment, and Louis, exhausted, fell motionless on the deck; but the bear, closing his paws tightly in a supreme agony, fell, dragging down the wretched Vasling, whose body was crushed under him.

Penellan hurried to Louis Cornbutte's assistance. No serious wound endangered his life; he had only lost his breath for a moment.

" Marie! " he said, opening his eyes.

" Saved! " replied Penellan. " Herming is lying there with a knife-wound in his stomach."

" And the bears——"

" Dead, Louis; dead, like our enemies! But for those beasts we should have been lost. Truly, they came to our succor. Let us thank Heaven! "

Louis and Penellan descended to the cabin, and Marie fell into their arms.

CHAPTER XVI
CONCLUSION

HERMING, mortally wounded, had been carried to a berth by Misonne and Turquiette, who had succeeded in getting free. He was already at the last gasp of death; and the two sailors occupied themselves with Nouquet, whose wound was not, happily, a serious one.

But a greater misfortune had overtaken Louis Cornbutte. His father no longer gave any signs of life. Had he died of anxiety for his son, delivered over to his enemies? Had he succumbed in presence of these terrible events? They could not tell. But the poor old sailor, broken by disease, had ceased to live!

At this unexpected blow, Louis and Marie fell into a said despair; then they knelt at the bedside and wept, as they prayed for Jean Cornbutte's soul. Penellan, Misonne, and Turquiette left them alone in the cabin, and went on deck. The bodies of the three bears were carried forward. Penellan decided to keep their skins, which would be of no little use; but he did not think for a moment of eating their flesh. Besides, the number of men to feed was now much decreased. The bodies of Vasling, Aupic, and Jocki, thrown into a hole dug on the coast, were soon rejoined by that of Herming. The Norwegian died during the night, without repentance or remorse, foaming at the mouth with rage.

Jean Cornbutte was buried on the coast. He had left his native land to find his son, and had died in these terrible regions! His grave was dug on an eminence, and the sailors placed over it a simple wooden cross.

From that day, Louis Cornbutte and his comrades passed through many other trials; but the lemons, which they found, restored them to health. Gervique, Gradlin, and Nouquet were able to rise from their berths a fortnight after these terrible events, and to take a little exercise.

Soon hunting for game became more easy and its results more abundant. The water-birds returned in large numbers. After the equinox, the sun remained constantly above the horizon. The eight months of perpetual daylight had begun. This continual sunlight, with the increasing though still quite feeble heat, soon began to act upon the ice.

Great precautions were necessary in launching the ship from the lofty layer of ice which surrounded her. She was therefore securely propped up, and it seemed best to await the breaking up of the ice; but the lower mass, resting on a bed of already warm water, detached itself little by little, and the ship gradually descended with it. Early in April she had reached her natural level.

In May the thaw became very rapid. The snow which

covered the coast melted on every hand, and formed a thick mud, which made it well-nigh impossible to land. Small heathers, rosy and white, peeped out timidly above the lingering snow, and seemed to smile at the little heat they received. The thermometer at last rose above zero.

Twenty miles off, the ice masses, entirely separated, floated towards the Atlantic Ocean. Though the sea was not quite free around the ship, channels opened by which Louis Cornbutte wished to profit.

On the 21st of May, after a parting visit to his father's grave, Louis at last set out from the bay. The hearts of the honest sailors were filled at once with joy and sadness, for one does not leave without regret a place where a friend has died. The wind blew from the north, and favored their departure. The ship was often arrested by ice-banks, which were cut with saws, icebergs not seldom confronted her, and it was necessary to blow them up with powder. For a month the way was full of perils, which sometimes brought the ship to the verge of destruction; but the crew were sturdy, and used to these dangerous exigencies. Penellan, Pierre Nouquet, Turquiette, Fidèle Misonne, did the work of ten sailors, and Marie had smiles of gratitude for each.

The *Jeune-Hardie* at last passed beyond the ice in the latitude of Jean-Mayen Island. About the 25th of June she met ships going northward for seals and whales. She had been nearly a month emerging from the Polar Sea.

On the 16th of August she came in view of Dunkirk. She had been signaled by the look-out, and the whole population flocked to the jetty. The sailors of the ship were soon clasped in the arms of their friends. The old curé received Louis Cornbutte and Marie with patriarchal arms, and of the two masses which he said on the following day, the first was for the repose of Jean Cornbutte's soul, and the second to bless these two lovers, so long united in misfortune.

THE END

The Pearl of Lima

OR

Martin Paz

The Pearl of Lima

CHAPTER I
THE "PLAZA MAYOR"

THE sun had just sunk behind the snowy peaks of the Cordilleras, and, although the beautiful Peruvian sky was being covered by the veil of night, the atmosphere was clear and refreshing in its balmy coolness. It was just the hour when a European might enjoy the climate, and with open veranda luxuriate in the grateful breeze.

The stars were beginning to appear and the promenaders betook themselves to the streets of Lima, where, protected merely by their light capes, they discussed the most trivial topics with the most profound gravity. The general direction of the throng was toward the grand square, the Plaza Mayor, the forum of the ancient " City of the Kings."

The same cool atmosphere which tempted the population to an evening stroll had the effect of bringing out the various hawkers, who threaded their way amidst the crowds shouting aloud the praises of their different wares. The women, wearing mantles which effectually concealed their faces, glided, as it were, between the groups of smokers. A few ladies there were in evening dress, with their *coiffure,* composed of their own luxuriant hair gracefully adorned with natural flowers; but these were lounging back in the wide barouches. The Indians were seen making their sullen way without once lifting their eyes, and indicating neither by gesture nor by word the rancorous envy that was gnawing at their spirit, a contrast altogether with the half-breeds, who, repudiated as themselves, protested more openly against their civil wrongs.

As for the Spaniards, those haughty descendants of Pizarro, they held their heads aloft as though they were still entitled to the homage of the days of old, when their ancestors had founded the city of the kings. They entertained supreme contempt alike for the Indians whom they had conquered, and for the half-breeds who had sprung from their own connection with the people of the New World. Like every other subjugated race, the Indians

109

chafed at their condition, and regarded with common antipathy not only the conquerors who had overturned the ancient empire of the Incas, but also the half-breeds, that upstart race, as arrogant as vulgar. With regard to these half-breeds, it may be asserted that they were Spaniards as far as their scorn of the Indians could make them so, while they were thorough Indians in the detestation in which they held the Spaniards. The two sentiments were about equally developed, and united in embittering their lives.

It was a party of the young half-breeds that was now seen clustering near the fine fountain that adorns the center of the Plaza Mayor. Each of them was wearing a "poncho," which consisted simply of an oblong piece of cotton, with an aperture in the middle to admit the head of the wearer, and nearly all of them were arrayed in loose trousers, gay with stripes of a thousand colors; on their heads they had broad-brimmed hats made of straw from Guayaquil. They gesticulated violently as they talked.

"You are right, André," said a little man named Millaflores, speaking in a most obsequious tone.

This Millaflores was a hanger-on, a sort of parasite of André Certa, a young half-breed, and the son of a wealthy merchant who had been killed in one of the late insurrections. Inheriting an ample fortune, André had sought by a lavish prodigality to surround himself with a bevy of friends from whom he exacted nothing more than the most servile deference.

"And what good, I should like to know," said André, raising his voice higher and higher as he spoke, "what good ever comes of these changes of government, and these everlasting *pronunciamentos* that are constantly agitating Peru. As long as there is no equality established, it matters little whether it be Gambarra or Santa Cruz that rules us."

"Well said! well said, indeed!" shrieked little Millaflores, who, in spite of the passing of a law for universal equality, could never be an equal to any man of spirit.

"Here am I," continued André Certa, "the son of a merchant, and how is it that I am not allowed a carriage drawn by anything better than mules! Whose ships were they but mine that brought prosperity into the land? And isn't an aristocracy of wealth far more than a match for all the empty titles of the grandees of Spain?"

" Disgraceful! " chimed in the voice of one of the young half-breeds; " utterly disgraceful! Just look there! there goes Don Fernando! see him how he drives along in his chariot drawn by horses! Don Fernando d'Aguillo! he can scarcely afford to buy a dinner for his coachman, and yet look at the air with which he lords it about the Plaza! Look, there's another of them! the Marquis Don Vegal! "

A splendid carriage at that moment turned into the Plaza, and proved in truth to belong to the Marquis Don Vegal, Chevalier of Alcantara, of Malta, and of Charles III. The nobleman had come out only to relieve the tedium of the evening, and with no thought of ostentation or display. As he sat with his head bent in anxious care, he paid no regard to the envious sneers with which the groups of half-breeds greeted him while his carriage and four dashed through the crowd.

" I hate that man," growled André Certa.

" Ah! you will not need to hate him long," replied one of the young men.

" Perhaps not," said André. " These lordlings have seen nearly the last of their luxuries, and have pretty well exhausted all their jewels and family plate."

" Yes, indeed; no one knows that better than yourself, familiar as you are with old Samuel the Jew."

" True; the old Jew's ledger shows plenty of credit and lots of debt, and his strong box is full to the hasp with the *débris* of the fine fortunes of the old aristocrats But the day isn't far off, and a jolly day it will be, when these Spaniards will all be beggars, like their own Cæsar de Bazan."

" Capital, André," put in Millaflores; " and then you will mount upon your own millions, and double them besides. But when do you marry old Samuel's daughter? Sarah is a true child of Lima, a Peruvian to the very tips of her fingers; nothing of the Jewess about her except her name."

" Oh, within a month," said André. " In another month there will not be a fortune in the land to compete with mine."

" But why," was the inquiry of one of the admiring group, " why don't you marry the daughter of some Spaniard who can boast a noble lineage? "

" Because I despise the race as much as I hate it," replied

André; but he did not think it necessary to confess that his acquaintanceship had been ignominiously rejected in every aristocratic circle to which he had endeavored to get an introduction.

At this instant André was unceremoniously jostled by a tall man with grisly hair, whose thick-set limbs indicated more than an ordinary amount of physical strength.

The man was an Indian, a native of the mountains; he wore a shirt of the coarsest serge, that, opening at the neck, revealed the shaggiest of bosoms; his short linen trousers were gaudy with green stripes, and his stone-colored stockings were fastened at the knee with crimson garters; a pair of glittering ear-rings hung far below the border of his hat.

After jostling André, the man stood and stared at him.

" You vile Indian! " exclaimed the assaulted half-breed, as he raised his hand to strike him.

His companions held him back, and Millaflores cried, " André, André! mind what you are about! "

" What does the wretched slave mean by daring to jostle me? " exclaimed André furiously.

" Never mind, he's only an idiot; it is Sambo! "

The Indian continued steadily staring at the man whom he had intentionally affronted. André, beside himself with rage, laid his hand upon the dagger which he carried in his belt, and was upon the point of attacking his aggressor, when a shrill cry, like the note of the Peruvian linnet, re-echoed above the tumult of the crowd, and in a moment Sambo had disappeared.

" Miserable coward! " ejaculated the furious André.

Millaflores gently begged him to control his passion, and leave the Plaza. The group of young men began to retire towards the lower end of the promenade.

The Plaza Mayor was still the scene of bustling animation. Night had come on, and gliding about with their identity completely disguised by their mantles, the women of Lima truly deserved their name of the " tapadas,"—the " concealed." The noise and tumult seemed ever to be increasing. The horse-guards, sentineled at the central gateway of the Viceroy's palace, had as much as they could do to retain their places undisturbed by the thronging of the busy crowd. Industry of every sort appeared to have found a general *rendezvous,* and the whole place was well-nigh given up to the exhibition of articles for sale. The lower story of the palace, and the very basement of the cathedral had been converted into shops, and the entire locality was thus transformed into a vast bazaar for all the varied products of the tropics.

Louder and louder waxed the noise; when all at once the bell from the cathedral tower tolled out the Angelus, and the tumult was completely hushed. The clamor of business was replaced by the whisperings of prayer. The ladies paused upon the promenade, and began to tell their beads.

During the interval of the suspended traffic, and while the mass of the people was still in the attitude of devotion, a young girl, accompanied by an old duenna, was trying to make her way through the thickest of the crowd. Angry remonstrances met the ears of both as their movements interrupted the prayers of those they passed. The girl wanted to stand and wait, but the undaunted duenna dragged her resolutely on. First some one would say, "What are these daughters of the devil doing?" and then another would ask, "Who is this cursed ballet-girl?" till at last, overwhelmed by confusion, the girl refused to advance a step.

At that instant a muleteer was proceeding to take her by the shoulder and force her on to her knees; but he had scarcely raised his hand for the purpose, when he was seized by a strong arm from behind, and felled to the ground. The incident, though it was quick as lightning, caused some confusion for a moment.

"Make your escape, young lady," said a voice, gently and respectfully, close to the girl's ear.

Pale with terror she cast a glance behind her, and saw a tall young Indian standing with folded arms and looking defiantly at the muleteer before him.

"Alas, alas!" cried the duenna, "we have got into trouble," and hurried the girl away.

Bruised by his fall the muleteer rose to his feet, but not deeming it prudent to demand satisfaction from an opponent of such resolute bearing as the young Indian, he retired towards his mules, muttering angry but useless threats as he went.

CHAPTER II
AN INDIAN RIVAL

THE town of Lima nestles as it were in the valley of the Rimac, at about nine miles from the mouth of the river. From east to west Lima is about two miles long, but not more than a mile and a quarter wide from the bridge to the walls. These walls, which are about twelve feet high, and ten feet thick at their base, are constructed of a peculiar kind of bricks, known as " adobes," dried in the sun.

This is the ancient " City of the Kings," founded in 1534 by Pizarro on the feast of the Epiphany. It has never ceased to be the scene of revolution. Formerly it was the chief emporium of America in the whole Pacific, to which it was opened by the port of Callao. The climate makes Lima one of the most agreeable places of residence in the New World. The wind never deviates from one of two directions; either it blows from the south-west, and brings with it the refreshing influence which it has gained in traversing the Pacific, or it comes from the south-east, invigorating and cheering with the coolness which it has gathered from the snowy summits of the Cordilleras. The nights, too, at Lima are delightful as elsewhere in the tropics; the dew which rises is a bountiful source of nutriment to a soil that is ever exposed to the rays of a cloudless sun.

On the evening in question, the girl, still attended by her duenna, arrived from the great square at the bridge of the Rimac without further misadventure. Her excitement was still intense, and made her start at every sound which brought to her imagination either the ringing of the muleteer's bells, or the whistle of an Indian.

The girl was Sarah, the daughter of Samuel the Jew, and she was now about to enter the house of her father. She was dressed in a dark-colored skirt plaited round the bottom in such close folds as to oblige her to take the very shortest steps, giving her that graceful movement which is so generally characteristic of the young women of Lima. The skirt was trimmed with lace and flowers, and was partially concealed by a silk mantle, the hood of which enveloped her head; stockings of fine texture, and pretty little satin slippers were visible below her becoming dress; bracelets of considerable value encircled her wrists, and her whole appearance afforded a charming illustration of what the Spaniards express so pointedly by their term " donayre."

Millaflores had only declared the truth when he had said that Sarah had nothing Jewish about her but her name; she was undeniably a type of the señoras whose beauty has commanded such universal homage.

The old duenna was a Jewess, with avarice and cupidity stamped indelibly upon her features; she was a devoted servant to Samuel, who knew what she was worth, and remunerated her accordingly.

Just at the moment that they entered the suburb of San Lazaro, a man, dressed as a monk, with his cowl over his head, passed them with a keen and scrutinizing look of inquiry. He was very tall, and had one of those commanding figures which seem at once to indicate repose and benevolence. It was Farther Joachim di Camarones. As he passed the girl he gave her a kindly smile of recognition; she glanced hastily at her companion, and merely acknowledge his greeting by a gentle movement of her hand.

" Has it come to this? " said the old woman, in a tone of annoyance, " isn't it enough to be insulted by these Christian dogs, and here you must be bowing and smiling to one of their priests! I suppose some day we shall see you take up a rosary, and go off to their fine services in church."

The girl colored as she replied, " You are indulging in strange conjectures."

" Strange! not more strange, I think, than your behavior. What would my master say if he knew all that has passed this evening? "

" It's no fault of mine, I should suppose," rejoined the girl, " if a brutal muleteer insults me in the street."

" I know very well what I mean," grumbled the old woman; " I wasn't alluding to any muleteer."

" Then," inquired Sarah, " do you blame that young Indian for taking my part against the crowd? "

" Ah! ah! but it isn't the first time the young fellow has crossed your path."

Fortunately for her, the maiden's face was covered by her mantilla, otherwise the evening shades would not have been deep enough to conceal the girl's flush of excitement from the inquisitive eye of the old domestic.

" But never mind the Indian now," continued the old

crone; " I will keep my eye on that business.   What troubles
me most now is that rather than interrupt those Christians
at their prayers, you should acutally stand still and wait
while they knelt, and I really believe you were going to
kneel too.   Ah! señora, if your father were to know that I
could allow you to insult your faith like that, he would not
be long in sending me adrift."

The girl however, heard nothing of the reproof.   The
very mention of the Indian had turned her thoughts into a
sweeter channel.   She recalled what was to her a provi-
dential interference on her behalf, and could not divest herself of a belief that her deliverer was still not far behind,
following in the shade.   There was a certain fearlessness in
her character that became her marvelously.   Proud she was
with the pride of a Spaniard, and if she felt her interest
awakened by the young Indian, it was chiefly because he,
too, was proud, and had not sought a glance of her eye as
an acknowledgment for his protection.

In truth, she was not far wrong in her surmise that the
Indian was not out of sight.   After his interference in her
defence, he had resolved to make her retreat entirely secure;
and accordingly, when the observers were dispersed, he
proceeded to follow her without being perceived.

A well-built man was Martin Paz, his figure being nobly
set off by the costume that he wore as an Indian of the
Mountains.   Below the wide brim of his straw hat clustered
massive locks of thick black hair which harmonized perfectly with his dark complexion.   His eyes were at once
brilliant and soft, and a well-formed nose rose above lips
so small as to be quite rare in any of his race.   He was of
the lineage of the courageous Manco-Capac, and in his veins
coursed the ardent blood that was capable of great achieve-
ments.

Martin Paz was attired in a poncho of many hues; from
his girdle was suspended one of those Malay daggers which
are ever formidable in a practiced hand, and seem to be
welded to the arm that wields them.   Had he been in North
America, by the wild borders of Lake Ontario, he would,
to a certainty, have been a chief of those wandering tribes
who fought so heroically against their English foes.

Martin was quite aware not only that Sarah was the
daughter of the wealthy Jew, but also, that she was be-

trothed to the rich half-breed, André Certa; he knew that
her birth, her social position, and her fortune, alike pro-
hibited her from ever having any relations with himself;
but overlooking all impossibilities, he gave free license to his
infatuation.

Plunged in his own reflections, he was hastening on his
way, when he was suddenly accosted by two other Indians.

"Martin Paz," said one of them, "don't you intend to go
to-night and meet our brothers in the mountains?"

"I shall be there," was Martin's curt reply.

"The schooner *Annunciation*," went on the other, "has
been seen off the heights of Callao. No doubt she will land
at the mouth of the Rimac, and our boats should be there to
disembark her cargo. Come, you must!"

"I know my own duty," said Martin.

"We speak to you here in Sambo's name."

"Yes," said Martin, "and I answer you in my own."

"How shall we account for your being here in San Lazaro at this extraordinary hour of the night?"

"I go where I please," was the only answer.

"In front of the Jew's house, too!"

"Such of my brethren as are offended at it may meet
me, and tell me of it this very night upon the hills."

The eyes of the three men flashed, but no more was said.
The two retreated towards the bank of the Rimac, and the
sound of their footsteps was soon lost in the distance.

Martin Paz had come quite alone to the residence of the
Jew. Like all the houses in Lima it was only two stories
high. The basement was built of bricks, and upon this was
raised another story composed of plaited canes, plastered
over and painted to match the walls below. This is a contrivance which is best adapted to resist the convulsions of
the frequent earthquakes. The roof was flat, and being
covered with flowers, it made a most fragrant and agreeable resort.

A broad gateway between two lodges gave access to a
courtyard within, but according to the custom of the place,
those lodges had no windows opening into the road.

The church clock had struck eleven, and there was the
deepest silence all around. And why is it that the Indian
lingers here before the walls? Only because a dim shadow
has been seen moving amidst those flowers, of which night

only hides the form, without depriving them of their delightful odors.

With an involuntary impulse Martin lifts his hands in ardent admiration. The dim figure starts and shrinks away as if in terror. Martin Paz withdraws his gaze from the roof to find himself face to face with André Certa.

"And for how long have the Indians been accustomed to pass their nights thus?" asked André, hot with rage.

"Ever since Indians have trodden the soil of their ancestors," sternly answered Martin Paz, without moving an inch. André advanced towards him.

"Wretch!" he angrily exclaimed, "will you not leave the place?"

"No!" cried Martin Paz, and in an instant daggers flashed in the right hands of both. They were of equal height, and seemed of equal strength. Quickly André raised his arm, but still more quickly it dropped; his poignard had met that of his antagonist, and he fell to the ground wounded in the shoulder.

"Help, help!" he shouted.

The gate of the Jew's house was quickly opened. Some half-breeds ran out hastily from an adjacent building; a part of them set out in pursuit of the Indian, who had at once made off, while the others attended the wounded man.

"Who is he?" asked a bystander. "If he is a sailor, he had better be carried off to the Hospital of St. Esprit; if he is an Indian, let him be taken to St. Anne's."

But at this point an old man approached, and having given a glance at the wounded André, said, "Take him into my house!" and then muttered to himself, "what strange piece of business is this?"

It was Samuel the Jew, who had thus recognized in the wounded man the intended husband of his daughter.

Meanwhile Martin Paz, favored by the darkness of the night and by his own fleetness, succeeded in escaping the hot pursuit of those who followed him. He was flying for his life. Could he only reach the open country, he would be safe; but the gates of the town, which were closed every night at eleven, would not be opened until four.

He reached the bridge, which he had crossed not long before. The half-breeds, with some soldiers who had joined them, pressed him closely from behind; an armed guard made its appearance right in front. Martin, unable either to advance or to retreat, bounded over the parapet, and leaped into the rapid stream that was dashing along its rocky bed. The soldiers rushed to the bank below the bridge to catch the fugitive as he reached the shore; but their effort was in vain. Martin Paz was nowhere to be seen.

CHAPTER III
THE JEW'S ANGER

ONCE safely lodged in the house of Samuel, and placed upon a couch that was quickly prepared for him, André Certa recovered his consciousness, and grasped the hand of the Jew. The surgeon who had been summoned was soon in attendance, and pronounced the wound to be unimportant, the shoulder having received the blow in such a way that the poignard had merely made a flesh wound; and there was no doubt that in a few days André would be convalescent.

When André found himself alone with Samuel he said to him, " I think you ought to block up the doorway that leads up to the terrace on the roof."

" Why? " rejoined the Jew. " What is there to be afraid of? "

" I don't think," continued André, " that it is right for Sarah to expose herself to the gaze of those Indians. It was from no burglar, it was simply from a rival that I received the cut that might have caused me serious injury: it was only by a miracle that I escaped."

" Ah! by the holy Bible! " shrieked the Jew, " you must be mistaken. My daughter will make you an accomplished wife, and I have always taken care that she shall do nothing that will damage your reputation."

André Certa lifted himself on to his elbow, and said significantly, " Are you not rather forgetting that I am to pay for Sarah's hand the price of no less than a hundred thousand piastres? "

" By no means," said the Jew with a greedy grin, " and I am quite ready to give you a receipt when I get the hard cash." And as he spoke he took from his portfolio a paper, of which André took no notice.

"There will be no bargain between us, Master Samuel, until Sarah becomes my wife; and that she won't be, if there is to be any difficulty about a rival. You know my object; I want to be a match for those haughty aristocrats, who now treat me with such vile contempt."

"And that is in your reach, André. Once married you will find the haughtiest Spaniards coming to your receptions."

"Where has your daughter been this evening?" asked André.

"To the synagogue with old Ammon, her companion."

"Why do you make your daughter attend those services?" said André. "What good can they be to her?"

"I am a Jew," replied the father, "and Sarah would not be my daughter if she did not fulfil the offices of our religion."

A villainous rascal was Samuel the Jew. Trading in commodities of any kind, however questionable, he was worthy to be a direct descendant of the Iscariot who betrayed his Master for thirty silver shekels. He had settled in Lima some ten years previously. Equally to please his taste and to serve his interests he had chosen a residence on the outskirts of the suburb of San Lazaro, where he applied himself to the most unscrupulous practices. Gradually his home assumed more and more of luxury, till at length he had a mansion sumptuous in its furniture, a numerous retinue of servants, and such splendid equipages as only belonged to men of unbounded affluence.

When Samuel first took up his abode in Lima his daughter was eight years of age. Already graceful and captivating in her manner, she was the very idol of the Jew. Her beauty increased with her age, and attracted universal admiration, and before long it was generally understood that André Certa, the rich half-breed, was desperately smitten with her; what would have appeared inexplicable was that the sum of a hundred thousand piastres should be the price of Sarah's hand, but that part of the contract was a secret. Besides, it was a part of old Samuel's nature to make a profit out of sentimental emotions just as though they were marketable products. Banker, usurer, broker, and shipowner, he had a faculty for doing business with everyone who came in his way. The schooner *Annunciation*, which

that very night was seeking to land at the mouth of the
Rimac, was his property.

Eagerly devoted as he was to the transactions of business, this man, with the persistence of his race, found time
to fulfil the religious offices of his creed with the most punc-
tilious regularity, and his daughter had been strictly trained
in the same faith; consequently, after André, in the course
of their conversation, had let it be seen how much the fact
displeased him, the old man sat for a time pensive and silent.
André at length broke the silence.

"You must be aware," he said, "that the motive under
which I contemplate marrying your daughter will compel
her to become a Catholic."

"True," answered Samuel in a mournful tone, "but, by
the holy Bible, as sure as Sarah is my daughter, Sarah will
be a Jewess still!"

At this moment the door was opened, and the steward of
the household entered.

"Has the assassin been arrested?" asked the Jew.

"We believe him dead," replied the steward.

"Dead!" exclaimed André, with a gesture of delight.

"So 'tis thought; he found himself upon the bridge with
us pursuing him from behind, and a guard of soldiers just
in front, and in order to escape, he jumped over the parapet
and flung himself into the stream."

"But what makes you think that he did not reach one of
the banks?" asked Samuel.

"Because the melting of the snow has swollen the stream
into a torrent," replied the steward. "Besides, we hurried
to each side of the river, but the man was never seen. The
sentinels have been left to watch the banks."

"Well," said the old man, "if he is drowned, he has only
executed just sentence upon himself. But did you recognize who he was?"

"Yes, it was Martin Paz, the Indian of the mountains."

"You mean the man who has now been so long watching
my daughter?"

"Of that I know nothing," said the servant indifferently.

The Jew then desired that Ammon, the old duenna,
should be sent to him, and the steward retired.

"Strange!" exclaimed the old man. "These Indians
have so many secret conspiracies; it ought to be known

how long this fellow has been carrying on his game."

By this time the duenna had entered the room, and stood waiting her master's pleasure.

" Does my daughter know anything of what has occurred to-night? " he inquired.

" I only know," was Ammon's reply, " that when I was roused by the clamor in the house, I hurried to the señora's room, and found her motionless with fright."

" Go on," he said impatiently, " tell me all."

" I pressed her to tell me the cause of her alarm; but she could not be induced to speak, and insisted upon going to bed; she would not allow me to attend her, and I was obliged to leave her to herself."

" This Indian, do you often meet him? "

" I can hardly say often," she replied, " but I must acknowledge that I know him very well by sight about the streets of San Lazaro, and this very evening he came to the señora's assistance in the Plaza Mayor."

" To her assistance! what do you mean? "

After the duenna had detailed the incident, the old Jew muttered wrathfully, " Is it true, then, that Sarah wanted to kneel down amongst those hateful Christians? " And then raising his voice, he threatened that Ammon should quit his service.

" Oh! forgive me, master, forgive me," was her deprecating cry.

" Out of my sight! " shouted Samuel harshly, and the duenna retreated in abashed confusion.

" There is no time to lose, you see," said André Certa. " it is high time that this marriage of ours should come off. But I want rest now, and shall be glad to be left alone."

The old man slowly retired; but before going to his own bed he wished to satisfy himself about the condition of his daughter, and accordingly he entered her apartment as gently as he could.

Sarah was sleeping very restlessly on a bed that was hung round with the richest of silk draperies. An elaborate lamp hung from the decorated boss upon the ceiling, and threw a soft light upon her face, whilst the window was opened just enough to admit the delicious perfume of the aloes and magnolias that were planted outside. With lavish luxury and consummate taste, articles of precious value were arranged about the chamber, and it might have been imagined that the mind of the sleeper was reveling amidst their beauties.

Her father came close to her side and bent down to watch her slumber. She was evidently agitated by some painful dream, and once the name of Martin Paz escaped her lips. The old man went to his room.

At break of day Sarah arose in eager haste. She summoned Liberta, an Indian attached to her service, and bade him saddle a horse for himself and a mule for her.

It was no long task for her to array herself in such a toilette as suited her design. A broad-brimmed hat, and her loosely-flowing tresses of black hair sheltered her face from observation, and the better to conceal the thoughts by which she was preoccupied, she placed a small perfumed cigarette between her lips.

She was no sooner mounted than she started off with her attendant across the country in the direction of Callao. The harbor was all alive with excitement, the coastguards having had to keep watch all night long upon the schooner, whose uncertain tackings indicated a fraudulent design. At one moment it would seem as though the vessel was waiting near the river's mouth for some suspicious-looking boats; but before they came alongside she was off again to avoid the long-boats belonging to the harbor. Many were the surmises about her destination. Some said that she had brought a body of Colombian troops, and intended to take possession of Callao, and to avenge the insult offered to the Bolivian soldiers who had been ignominiously expelled from Peru. Others maintained that she was merely a schooner driving a contraband trade in European wool.

To Sarah these speculations were all indifferent. She had only come to the port as a pretext, and now returned to Lima, which she reached at the point nearest to the river. Following the banks of the stream she went as far as the bridge, whence she noticed the groups of soldiers and half-breeds gathered along shore.

Liberta had made the girl acquainted with the events of the night. In obedience to her orders he now inquired further particulars from some of the soldiers, and learnt that although Martin Paz was doubtless drowned, his body had not yet been recovered.

Ready to faint, Sarah had to gather up all her strength of mind to avoid giving way to bitter grief. Amongst the people who were wandering up and down the bank she caught sight of a wild-looking Indian, whom she immediately recognized as Sambo. Passing close beside him, she heard him mournfully exclaim, "Alas! alas! they have killed the son of Sambo! My son is dead!"

The girl presently recovered her self-possession, and making a sign to Liberta to follow her, and not troubling herself as to whether she was observed or not, she directed her way to the church of St. Anne, and having left her mule in Liberta's care, she entered the Catholic house of prayer, and after she had asked for Father Joachim, she knelt upon the flagstones and prayed for the soul of Martin Paz.

CHAPTER IV
THE MARQUIS DON VEGAL

EXCEPTING Martin Paz there was scarcely another man in all the world to whom the torrent of the Rimac would not have proved a sure destruction. But his strength of body was amazing, and his strength of will resistless; and he was, moreover, greatly aided by that imperturbable *sang froid* which is characteristic of the free Indians of the New World.

Knowing intuitively that the soldiers would reckon on capturing him below the bridge, where the stream was too powerful to be combated, he put forth all his energy, and succeeded in stemming the torrent the other way. He found the resistance less in the side-currents, and contrived to reach the bank, where he concealed himself behind a cluster of mangroves.

But what would happen next? Soon the soldiers would change their tactics and explore the river upwards; and then what would be his chance of escape? His determination was soon taken; he would re-enter the town and find a refuge there.

To elude the observation of any of the residents who might be out late, it would perhaps have been best to take the wider streets. But he could not resist the impression that he was watched, and he dared not hesitate. All at once he caught sight of a house still brilliantly lighted up; the

gateway was open to allow the carriages to pass out, and the
very *élite* of the Spanish aristocracy were thence returning
to their own homes.

Without being seen he entered the house, and the gates
were almost immediately closed behind him. He hurried
on, ascending a cedar staircase adorned with costliest tapes-
try, and after passing through apartments still brilliantly
illuminated, but absolutely empty, he found a place of con-
cealment in a dark chamber beyond.

Before long the lamps were all extinguished, and silence
reigned throughout the house. Martin ventured from his
hiding-place to reconnoiter the situation. He found that
the window of the room opened on to a garden below;
escape seemed to him to be quite practicable, and he was on
the point of leaping down when he was startled by a voice
behind him: " Stop, señor, you have forgotten to take the
diamonds that I left on the table."

He looked back. There stood a haughty-looking man
pointing to a jewel case that lay before him.

Thus assailed, Martin approached the Spaniard, who was
still standing without moving a muscle, and drawing a dagger, which he pointed towards his own heart, he said, with
a voice trembling with agitation, " Repeat your words, and
you find me dead at your feet! "

Dumb with amazement, the Spaniard gazed steadily at
the Indian, and felt an involuntary sympathy rising up
within him. He went to the window and shut it gently;
then, turning to the Indian, who had let his dagger fall to
the ground, he asked him who he was, and whence he had
come.

" I am Martin Paz. I was escaping the pursuit of the
soldiers. I had wounded a half-breed with my dagger. I
was defending myself. The man I struck is betrothed to
the girl I love. It rests with you to save me, or to surrender me, as you think best."

The Spaniard stood in silent thought. After a while he
said, " To-morrow I am going to the baths of Chorillos.
If it will answer your purpose, go with me. For a time,
at least, you will be safe, and you will not have to complain
of any lack of hospitality from the Marquis Don Vegal."

Martin Paz bent his head in tacit assent.

" But now," continued Don Vegal, " you had better take

a few hours' rest. No one in the world will suspect your hiding place."

The Spaniard retired to his own apartment. Martin was deeply touched by the generosity with which he had met, and, relying on the good faith of the marquis, resigned himself to a peaceful slumber.

Next morning, at daybreak, the marquis gave his orders for starting, but previously arranged to have an interview with Samuel the Jew. First of all, however, he went to the early morning mass. The Peruvian aristocracy were always constant in their attendance at this service. From its earliest foundation Lima had always been pre-eminently Catholic. Besides its numerous churches, it counted at that time no less than twenty-two convents, seventeen monasteries, and four *pensions* for ladies who had not actually taken the veil. To each of these separate establishments was attached its own chapel, so that altogether there could not be less than a hundred places of worship, in which about eight hundred secular and regular priests, and three hundred nuns, besides lay brotherhoods and sisterhoods, devoted themselves to the offices of religion.

As he entered St. Anne's the eye of the marquis was attracted by the kneeling figure of a girl, who was weeping as she prayed. So great was her agitation, that he could not repress his sympathy, and was about to address her in some words of kind encouragement, when Father Joachim whispered, " Do not disturb her, marquis, I pray you! "

And then he beckoned to the girl, who followed him into a dim and empty chapel. Don Vegal made his way to the altar and attended mass, but could not dismiss from his memory the image of the girl who had so strangely arrested his attention.

Upon his return home he found Samuel the Jew awaiting his commands. Samuel seemed to have entirely forgotten the incidents of the past night; the prospect of gain had made him quite oblivious of all besides, and gave a keen vivacity to the expression of his face. " I await your lordship's commands," he said.

" I must have thirty thousand piastres within an hour."

" Thirty thousand! " cried the Jew. " How is it possible? By our holy David, I should have more difficulty in finding them than you seem to think."

Without taking any notice of what the usurer was saying, the marquis explained that, besides his valuable cases of jewels, he had a piece of land near Cusco that he would sell at a price far below its real value.

"Land!" exclaimed Samuel. "Why, it's land that ruins us! We can't get any labor to till the land since the Indians have withdrawn to the mountains. Land! why, its produce does not pay its expenses!"

"But, tell me," said the marquis, "at how much do you value the diamonds alone?"

The old man drew from his pocket a small pair of jeweler's scales, and proceeded to weigh the gems with an air of minute precision, at the same time, according to his habit, keeping up a running current of depreciation.

"Diamonds! yes, they are diamonds; but see how badly set! One might as well bury his money in the ground. Look here! what a stone! no purity about it. I can assure your lordship that I shall find it very difficult to get a customer at all for this costly purchase. Perhaps if I send them to the States, the Northerners will buy them in order to get rid of them to some English purchaser. No doubt they will make a good profit out of them, but then the loss would all fall upon me. Upon my word, your lordship, you must be satisfied with ten thousand piastres. It seems a little, but——"

"I have already told you that ten thousand piastres are of no use to me," said the marquis, with an air of profound contempt.

"Not one half-real more. I could not afford it," rejoined the inflexible Jew.

"Then take the caskets; only let me have the sum I ask, and give it me at once. Thirty thousand I must have, and you shall have a bond upon this house of mine. Substantial, is it not?"

"Ah, your lordship, but there are so many earthquakes here. One never knows who may be alive and who may be dead from one moment to another, nor yet which houses may stand, or which may fall."

And all the time the Jew was talking he kept stamping with his foot upon the inlaid floor, as if to test its real stability. He paused for an instant, and then resumed, "However, to oblige your lordship, it shall be as you wish; although just now I am indisposed to part with ready cash, as I am marrying my daughter to the young squire, André Certa. Do you know him?"

"Not at all. But lose no time: our bargain is made. Take the caskets, and give me the gold."

"Would your lordship wish for a receipt?" asked Samuel.

The marquis condescended to give no reply, and left the room.

"Arrogant Spaniard!" muttered the Jew, and gnashed his teeth in wrath. "Would that I could crush your pride as I can ruin your estate! By Solomon! 'tis clever practice to make one's interests and one's wishes agree so well."

After leaving the Jew, the marquis had gone to Martin Paz. He found him in a state of the gloomiest dejection.

"Well! how now?" he said kindly.

"Ah, señor! the daughter of that Jew is the girl I love."

"A Jewess!" exclaimed the marquis, in a tone of abhorrence which he could ill disguise; but compassionating the sorrow of the Indian, he only said, "Now then, it is time to start; we will talk about these things as we go along."

Within an hour Martin Paz, after changing his clothes, left the town in company with the Marquis Don Vegal, who took no other attendants.

The sea-baths of Chorillos are two leagues distant from Lima. It is a parish inhabited by Indians, and has a pretty church. During the warm season it is a favorite resort of all the *élite* of Lima, for the public gaming-tables, which are forbidden in the city, are here kept open throughout the summer. The ladies especially show a remarkable enthusiasm for this amusement, and during the season many a wealthy knight has seen his large fortune pass away into the hands of his fair opponents.

Just at that time Chorillos was almost deserted, and Don Vegal and Martin Paz, in their retired cottage on the seashore, were free to contemplate in peaceful solitude the wide expanse of the Pacific.

The Marquis Don Vegal, a scion of one of the most ancient Spanish families in Peru, was the only surviving representative of that noble lineage of which he was so justly proud. Traces of the deepest melancholy were ever visible on his countenance, and although, during a considerable portion of his life, he had been engaged in political affairs, the perpetual revolutions, instigated as they had been by motives of mere personal aggrandizement, so disgusted him with the outer world, that he withdrew from it altogether, and passed his time in a seclusion from which only matters of the strictest etiquette could ever induce him to emerge.

Little by little his fortune, once so immense, was dwindling away; he could with difficulty obtain credit for advances of capital, so that not only had his estates fallen into a condition of great neglect, but he had been obliged to mortgage them very heavily. The prospect of ultimate ruin stared him in the face, but in spite of the hopeless aspect of his affairs he never flinched for a moment. The heedlessness, characteristic of the Spanish race, together with the weariness induced by his objectless life, combined to make him utterly indifferent to the future. He had no domestic ties to bind him to the world; a beloved wife and charming little daughter, the sole objects of his affection, had been snatched from him by a melancholy fate; and he was contented passively to take his chance and await the chapter of events.

But cold and deadened as he had deemed his heart to be, his contact with Martin Paz had done something to awaken him from his habitual lethargy. The fiery temperament of the Indian did something towards rekindling the smouldering ashes of the Spaniard's sensitiveness. The marquis was worn out by his association with his fellow-countrymen, in whom he had no confidence; he was disgusted with the insolent half-breeds who were ever encroaching upon the prerogatives of his own order; and so he seemed to turn for relief to that primitive race which had fought so valiantly to defend its soil against the soldiers of Pizarro.

According to the information which the marquis received, it was currently reported that the Indian was dead. Worse than death, however, it appeared to Don Vegal that Martin Paz should ally himself in matrimony to a Jewess, and accordingly he resolved to rescue him doubly by allowing the daughter of Samuel to be married without interference to André Certa. He could not do otherwise than observe the depression which weighed upon Martin, and he hoped to divert him from his melancholy by avoiding the topic entirely, and by calling his attention to indifferent matters.

One day, however, distressed at noticing the saddened preoccupation of his guest, he could not resist asking him, "How is it that the innate nobility of your nature does not revolt against what must be so deep a degradation? Remember your ancestor, the redoubtable Manco-Capac; his patriotism exalted him to the highest rank of heroes, and no one with a noble part to play should condescend to an ignoble passion. Do you not burn to regain the independence of your soil?"

"Ah, señor," said the Indian, "we never lose sight of that glorious enterprise, and the day is not far off when my brethren will rise *en masse* to accomplish it!"

"I understand to what you refer," replied the marquis; "you are thinking of that secret war which you are planning in the retirement of the mountains; you are going to descend in full array, and at a concerted signal pounce upon the town below. Yes, you may come, but you will come, as you have always come, only to be vanquished. You have not the faintest chance of making good your hold amidst the continual revolutions of which Peru must be the scene,—revolutions which elevate the half-breeds to the detriment alike of Indians and of Spaniards."

"Nay, but we will save our country!" was Martin's eager remonstrance.

"Save it? yes, you may; if only you comprehend your proper part. But listen to me for a moment. I would speak to you as tenderly as though you were my son. I tell you, although I own it with the deepest sorrow, that we Spaniards are degenerate sons of a once powerful race: our energy is gone, and we entirely lack the vigor to regain the supremacy we have lost. But it rests with you to prevail; and prevail you can if you will only crush the mischievous spirit of Americanism which is refusing to tolerate the settlement of foreigners as colonists amongst us. Be sure of this: there is only one policy that can save the old Peruvian Empire; you must have a European immigration. The intestine war which you are contemplating can effect no good at all; it will only trample out every grade but the one you want to extinguish. Nothing can be done except you frankly stretch out the hand of welcome to the laboring population of the Old World."

" Indians, señor," replied Martin Paz, " must ever be the
sworn foes of strangers, let them come whence they will.
Indians will never tolerate the claims of foreigners to plant
their footsteps upon their soil or to breathe their mountain
air. My control over them is of such a character that it
would not last a moment longer than I should denounce
death to every oppressor of their liberty. It must be borne
in mind, too," he continued, in a tone of mournful despon-
dency, " that I am myself a fugitive with not three hours to
live if I were to venture into the streets of Lima."

" Lima!" exclaimed the marquis, "you must promise me
at least that you will not trust yourself in Lima!"

" Were I to pledge myself to that," said Martin, " I should
be disguising the true intention of my heart."

Don Vegal sat and mused in silence. There was no room
to doubt that the Indian's passion was growing more intense from day to day, and the marquis knew that if he
should presume to enter Lima he would to a certainty be exposing himself to an immediate death. What could he do
but resolve by any and all means at his command to hurry
on the marriage of the young Jewess to André Certa.

To convince himself of the true state of affairs the marquis rose betimes one morning and made his way from Chorillos back into the town. He was there informed that
André Certa had so far recovered from his wound that he
was about again, and that his approaching marriage was the
subject of general gossip.

Desirous of seeing the maiden who had so completely
captivated Martin Paz, the Marquis Don Vegal directed his
steps towards the Plaza Mayor at the evening hour, when
the throng was invariably very great, and on his way encountered his old friend, Father Joachim. The monk was
extremely astonished at being informed that Martin Paz was
still alive, and nothing could exceed the eagerness with
which he undertook to keep a watch on behalf of the young
Indian, and to acquaint the marquis with any intelligence
which might be of interest to him.

While the two were conversing, the attention of the marquis was arrested by a young girl enveloped in a black mantle, who was reclining on the low seat of a barouche.

" Who is that handsome young lady?" he inquired of
Father Joachim.

"That is old Samuel's daughter, the girl who is on the point of marrying André Certa," said the monk.

"*That* the daughter of a Jew!" involuntarily exclaimed Don Vegal; but he restrained further expression of his astonishment, shook hands with his friend, and retraced his way to Chorillos.

His surprise bewildered him still more when he came to consider that perchance she was not really a Jewess; he had recognized her as the girl whom he had seen kneeling in prayer within the Church of St. Anne.

CHAPTER V
THE PLOT BETRAYED

All this time, however, a very unusual agitation was going on amongst the Indians; those of them who resided in the town keeping up a vigorous communication with those who habitually made their homes amongst the mountains. They seemed for a time to have shaken off the dullness of their native apathy. No longer lounging wrapped in their ponchos and basking in the sunshine, they were ever and again hurrying to and fro in the direction of the open country; they greeted one another significantly as they met; they were ever making mysterious signs of mutual recognition, and continually held their meetings in out-of-the-way, second-rate hotels, where they could carry on their conferences without any risk of being observed.

This unusual commotion was for the most part obvious in one of the loneliest quarters of the town. At the corner of a street there was a dejected tenement, only one story high, the miserable appearance of which could not fail to attract observation. It was a kind of tap-room, of the lowest description, kept by an old Indian woman, who found her customers entirely among the most abject of the poor, who bought her beer made from fermented maize, or, failing that, contented themselves with a decoction of sugar-canes.

It was only at certain hours that there was any gathering of Indians at that spot, the signal of meeting being a long pole displayed on the roof of the building. But whenever notice was given there was soon a motley assemblage of the lowest class of the natives; there were cabriolet-drivers, muleteers, and carmen hurrying to the place of rendezvous, without loitering for a moment outside. The hostess was all on the alert, and, leaving the care of her counter to the charge of a servant-maid, hastened herself to give her best attention to her habitual guests.

A few days after the disappearance of Martin Paz there was a concourse larger than usual collected in the large room of the inn. The apartment was dim with clouds of tobacco-smoke, and it was with much difficulty that any-one of the *habitués* of the place could be distinguished from another. Altogether there were about fifty Indians congregated around the long table, some of whom were chewing a kind of tea-leaf mixed with a morsel of fragrant earth, while others were drinking fermented liquor from huge cans; but none of them seemed so much absorbed in their own doings as to prevent them from attending to the speech in which an old Indian was addressing them.

This Indian was no other than Sambo, and the whole assembly appeared to be following him with an eager interest. He looked with a keen scrutiny round the circle of his audience, and, after a brief pause, continued his appeal.

" The Children of the Sun can now discuss their own affairs quite unmolested. No perfidious spy can overhear them here. All round about are friends who, disguised as wandering street-singers, attract the passers-by, and prevent all interruption, so that now we may enjoy an uncontrolled and ample liberty.

And while he spoke the notes of a mandolin were heard thrumming in the thoroughfare hard by. Certified as to their security, the whole gathering of Indians prepared to pay a yet closer attention to the words of Sambo, who manifestly enjoyed their largest confidence. One of the party, however, interrupted him by asking abruptly: " Can Sambo give us any tidings of Martin Paz? "

" None whatever," he replied; " nor can I tell you whether he is alive or dead: the Great Spirit alone knows that. But I am expecting some of our brethren back who have been exploring the river down to its very mouth, and they perchance will have something to relate about the lost body of your chief."

"Ay, he might be a good leader," said an Indian named Manangani, with the fierce, bold manner that belonged to him; "but why was he wanting in his duty, and absent from his post on the very night that the schooner arrived with our arms?"

The question elicited no reply. Sambo hung his head in silence.

"Are our brethren aware," continued Manangani, "that there was an exchange of shots that night between the schooner and the coastguards, and do they know that the capture of the *Annunciation* would have been fatal to our enterprise?"

A murmur of assent ran through the assembly.

Sambo now took up the conversation, saying that all who would wait to judge the matter would be welcome.

"And who knows," he said, "whether my son shall not some day reappear? Be patient still. Even now the arms which we received from Sechura are in our keeping; safe they are in the mountain recesses of the Cordilleras, and ready to fullfil their work when you are prepared to do your duty."

"And what shall hinder us?" exclaimed a young Indian; "our weapons are sharpened, and we only bide our time."

"The hour will come," said Sambo; "but do our brethren know on whom the blow ought first to fall?"

The voice of one of the party was heard protesting that the first to perish ought to be the half-breeds who had treated them so insolently, chastising them like restive mules.

"Not so," declared another; "the first that we should strike should be the appropriators of the soil we tread."

"Mistaken are ye altogether!" shouted Sambo, with a voice raised in eagerness. "You must let your blows fall first in another quarter. It is not those of whom you speak that have dared for three centuries to plant their foot upon our ancestral soil; rich as they are, it is not they who have dragged the descendants of Manco-Capac to the tomb. No; rather 'tis the haughty Spaniards who are the true conquerors, and who have reduced you to the condition of being their very slaves. Their riches may have gone, but their authority survives, and they it is who, in spite of any emancipation that should give liberty to Peru, still trample our natural rights beneath their feet. Let us forget what we are, just that for once we may remember what our fathers were."

"True! true!" was the shout that burst forth from many a voice in the excited company.

Then ensued a few moments of silent consideration, when Sambo proceeded to make inquiries of some of the conspirators and to satisfy himself that their allies in Cusco and throughout Bolivia were ready to rise as one man.

His enthusiasm soon again broke out in speech. "And our brethren on the mountains, brave Manangani, only let them cherish in their souls a hatred such as yours, and arm themselves with your courage, too, and they shall fall upon Lima as an avalanche might come crashing down from the Cordilleras."

"Sambo shall not need to complain," said Manangani; "their firmness will not fail them at the proper time. Go but a few yards beyond the town and you shall find groups of eager Indians fired with the passion of revenge. In the gorges of San Cristoval and the Amancäes many a one beneath his poncho wears his poignard hanging in his belt, and only waits to have the rifle trusted to his hand. Never will they forget to exact the vengeance that is due from the Spaniards for their defeat of Manco-Capac."

"Good!" replied Sambo; "it is the God of hatred that inspires your lips. My brethren shall soon know what their chiefs have decided. All that Gambarra wants now is to consolidate his power; Bolivar has retired; Santa Cruz has been chased away, and we can act in perfect safety. Wait but a few days and our adversaries will be taking their pleasure at the coming festival of the Amancäes. Then will be our time; then must we set ourselves in motion, and the summons must be heard even to the remotest village of Bolivia."

Three Indians at this moment entered the room. Sambo received them with the eager inquiry:

"Well, what news? Is he found?"

"No," replied one of the three; "the body is nowhere to be found. Though we have searched every foot of the river bank, and sent the most skillful of our divers down to search the depths, we find no trace of Sambo's son. Doubtless he has perished in the waters of the Rimac."

"Have they then killed him? Is he lost? Woe, woe to them if they have slain my son!" Then, repressing his passion, he added, "Let my brothers now go quietly away. Go ye away to your place, but be on your guard and ready for the call."

All the Indians gradually took their departure, leaving Sambo and Manangani alone behind.

"Do you know," asked Manangani, "what was the motive that took your son that night to the quarter of San Lazaro? Are you sure of him?"

"Sure of him!" said Sambo, re-echoing the words, with a flash of indignant wrath in his eyes beneath which Manangani involuntarily recoiled, "sure of him! If Martin Paz should be a traitor to his friends, I would first slay every soul to whom he had given his friendship; nay, I would not spare them to whom he had yielded his dearest love; and then I would kill him; and, last of all, I would kill myself. Perish everything beneath the sun rather than dishonor shall befall our race."

His fervid speech was interrupted by the hostess bringing in a letter addressed to him.

"Who gave you this?" he asked.

"I cannot tell," replied the woman; "it was left, apparently by design, as if forgotten by one of the men who have been drinking at one of the tables."

"Have any but Indians been in here?" he inquired.

"None whatever but Indians," was her prompt reply.

As soon as the woman had gone he unfolded the document and read it aloud: "A young girl has been praying for Martin Paz. She cannot forget one who has imperiled his life for the sake of hers. Has Sambo any tidings of his son? If he has news of him, let him bind a scarlet band around his arm. There are eyes ever on the watch to see him pass."

Crumpling up the paper, he exclaimed: "Unhappy fool! to be entangled by the fascinations of a pretty girl!"

"Who is she?" inquired Manangani.

"No Indian maid," said Sambo, "some dainty damsel full of airs. Ah, Martin Paz, you are beside yourself! I know you not!"

"Do you mean to do what the woman asks?"

"No!" said the Indian vehemently, "let her abandon

all hope of setting eyes upon my son again, and let her die in ignorance!" And while he spoke he angrily tore the paper into fragments.

"It must have been an Indian who brought the letter," observed Manangani.

"Not one of our party. It is known well enough that I am often here, but I shall not come again. Now do you return to the mountains. I will keep watch in the town. The feast day comes, and we shall see whether it be a festival of rejoicing for the oppressors or the oppressed." With this parting direction the two Indians each departed on his own way.

The plot of the Indians had been deeply laid, and the time for its execution was adroitly chosen. The population of Peru was reduced to a comparatively small number of Spaniards and half-breeds. From the forests of Brazil, from the mountains of Chili, from the plains of La Plata, the hordes of Indians had been summoned, and would find it an easy task to cover the whole territory which was to be the theater of revolution. Once let the larger towns, Lima, Cusco, and Puno, fall into their hands, and victory was all their own. There was no fear of the Colombian troops, who had recently been driven out by the Peruvian government, returning to assist their adversaries in the hour of their necessity.

And it can hardly be doubted that this revolutionary movement would have resulted in entire success if its intention had been confided to none but Indian breasts: among them there was no fear of treachery.

But they knew not that there was a man who already had obtained a private audience with Gambarra, and had apprized him that the schooner *Annunciation* had been unlading firearms of every description into the canoes and pirogues of the Indians at the mouth of the Rimac; they knew not that that man had gone to claim a reward from the Peruvian Government for the very service of exposing their own proceedings.

A double game was this. The man who for a large payment had chartered his ship to Sambo for the conveyance of the arms, had gone at once to the president and betrayed the existence of the conspiracy.

The man was Samuel the Jew.

As soon as he was restored to health, André Certa, still believing in the death of Martin Paz, began to hurry on his marriage. His intended bride continued to regard him with the most complete indifference; but this did not occasion him any concern; he regarded her solely as a costly article for which he had to pay the handsome price of 100,000 piastres.

It must be alleged that André had no confidence at all in the Jew, and he was right in entertaining mistrust. If the contract had been void of honesty, so were the contractors void of principle. Accordingly André was now anxious for a private interview with Samuel, and for that purpose took him for a day to Chorillos, where he also hoped to have the chance of trying a little gambling before his marriage.

The gaming-tables had been opened at the baths a few days after the marquis's arrival, and ever since they had been the means of keeping up an incessant traffic along the road to Lima. Some came on foot, who returned with the luxury of a carriage; while others came only fairly to exhaust the remnant of a shattered fortune.

Neither Don Vegal nor Martin Paz took any share in the play; the restlessness of the young Indian was caused by a far nobler game. After their evening walks Martin would take leave of the marquis, and, going to his own room, would lounge with his elbows on the window-sill, and spend hours in silent reverie.

The marquis ever and again recalled to his recollection the young girl whom he had seen praying in the Catholic church, but he did not venture to entrust the secret to his guest, although he took occasion little by little to acquaint him with the essentials of the Christian faith. He hesitated to allude to the girl, because he was fearful of reviving the very interest that he was anxious to allay. It was necessary that the Indian should renounce every hope of obtaining the hand of Sarah. Only let the police, he thought, abandon their search for Martin, and his protector did not doubt that in the course of time he could procure him an introduction into the first circle of Peruvian society.

But Martin Paz would not surrender himself to despair

without assuring himself of the hopelessness of his chance. He resolved at all risks to know the actual destiny of the young Jewess. Screened from suspicion by his Spanish attire, he thought he might enter into the gambling-halls, and so hear the conversation of those who habitually frequented them. André Certa was a person of sufficient note to make his marriage, as it drew near, a topic of considerable talk.

One evening, therefore, instead of turning his steps towards the seashore, the Indian bent his way towards the high cliffs on which the principal houses in Chorillos were built, and entered a house that was approached by a large flight of stone steps. This was the gambling-house.

The day had been trying to more than one of the people of Lima. Some of them, worn out by the fatigue of the preceding night, were reposing on the ground, covered with their ponchos. The other gamblers were seated before a large table covered with green baize, and divided into four compartments by two lines that cut each other at right angles in the middle. Each of these compartments was marked with either the letter A., or the letter S., the initial letters of the Spanish words " asar," and " suerte," hazard and chance. The players put their money upon whichever of the letters they chose, a croupier held the stakes, and threw two dice upon the table, and the combined readings of the points determined whether A. or S. was the winner.

At this particular moment there was a general animation, and one half-breed could be noticed persevering against ill-luck with a feverish determination.

" Two thousand piastres! " he exclaimed.

The croupier shook the dice, and a muttered curse fell from the player's lips.

" Four thousand piastres! " he said.

But again he lost.

Protected by the shadows of the hall, Martin Paz caught a glimpse of the player's face. It was André Certa, and close beside him stood the Jew Samuel. " There," said Samuel, " that's play enough. The luck is all against you to-day."

" Curse the luck! " said André impetuously, " it does not matter to you."

The Jew whispered in the young man's ear: " It may

not matter to me; but to you it matters much, and you should desist from the practice for the few days before your marriage."

"Eight thousand piastres!" was the only reply that André made, as he laid his stake upon the S.

"A. wins," was the immediate decision of the dice, and the half-breed's blaspheming oaths were hardly covered by the croupier's summons, "Make your game, gentlemen; make your game."

Taking a roll of notes from his pocket, André was on the point of hazarding a still larger sum; he was placing them on the table, and the croupier was already shaking his dice box.

The Jew bent his head again towards the ear of André, and said: "You will have nothing left to-night to close our bargain. Everything will then be broken off."

André shrugged his shoulders, and uttered an ejaculation of rage; but he took up the money he had staked, and went out of the room.

"You may go on now," said Samuel, addressing the croupier; "you may ruin that gentleman if you like, but not until after his marriage."

The croupier bowed obsequiously. The Jew was the originator and proprietor of the gaming-house. Wherever there was gold to be won, he was sure to be found.

Following the young half-breed out, he overtook him upon the stone steps, and telling him that he had matters of great importance to communicate to him, asked where they might converse in uninterrupted security.

"Where you please!" said André, with abrupt discourtesy.

"Let me advise you, señor," said Samuel, "not to let your bad temper interfere with your future advantage. My secret is not to be revealed within the best closed doors; no, nor yet in the most secluded wilderness. It is a secret for which you think you are paying me a good high price, but let me assure you it is well worth keeping."

While they were thus talking they came to the spot where the bathing-houses were erected; but they had no idea how they were being overlooked and overheard by Martin Paz, who had glided after them like a serpent.

"Let us take a boat," said André, "and put out to sea."

He then loosened a light boat from its moorings on the shore, and flinging some money to its owner, he made Samuel get in, and pushed off into the open water.

No sooner did Martin Paz observe the boat leave the shore than, concealed by a projecting rock, he hastily undressed, and taking the precaution to fasten on his belt, to which he attached a poignard, he swam with all his strength in the same direction. By this time the sun had sunk below the horizon, and the obscurity of twilight enveloped both sea and sky.

One thing Martin had forgotten. He did not call to mind that the waters of these latitudes were infested with sharks of the most ferocious kind; but, plunging recklessly into the fatal flood, he made good his way till he was near enough to the boat just to catch the voices of the two as they spoke.

"But what proof am I to give the father of the girl's identity?" were the first words he heard André say.

"Proof! why, you must detail the circumstances under which he lost his child."

"What were the circumstances?" asked André.

"Listen, and you shall hear," replied the Jew.

Martin Paz could only by an effort keep his position within ear-shot of the boat, and what he heard he failed to comprehend.

The Jew proceeded to say: "It was in Chili, at Concepcion, that Sarah's father lived. He is a nobleman that you already know, and his wealth was according to his rank. He was obliged, by business of a pressing nature, to come to Lima. He came alone, leaving behind his wife and a little daughter only five months old. In every respect the climate of Peru was agreeable to him, and he sent for his lady to join him there. Bringing with her only a few trusty servants, she embarked on the *San José*, of Valparaiso. On that ship it chanced that I was myself a passenger. The *San José* was bound to put into harbor at Lima; but just off the point of Juan Fernandez she was exposed to a terrific hurricane, which disabled her, and laid her upon her beam-ends. The whole of the crew, and the passengers, betook themselves to the long-boat. The marchioness refused to enter the boat, but clasping her infant in her arms, resolved at all hazards to remain where she was. I remained with her. The long-boat made off, but before it had proceeded a hundred fathoms from the ship, it was swallowed up in the angry waters. The two of us remained alone. The storm came on with increasing fury. As I had not my property on board, I was not reduced to a condition of absolute despair. The *San José*, with five feet of water in her hold, drove upon the rocks and was dashed to pieces. The lady with her child was thrown into the sea. It was my fortune to be able to rescue the little girl, although I saw the mother perish before my eyes; and with the child in my arms, I contrived to reach the shore."

"Are these details all correct?" asked André.

"Yes, to the most minute particular. The father will not deny them. Ah! I did a good day's work when I earned that 100,000 piastres which you are going to pay me."

Perplexed beyond measure, Martin could not suppress the ejaculation, "What does all this mean?"

"Here," said André, "here is your money."

"Thanks!" replied Samuel, eagerly pocketing the cash, "and here is your receipt. I guarantee to return you twice the sum if you do not find yourself a member of one of the noblest Spanish families."

Martin Paz was more bewildered than ever. He could give no meaning to what he heard. The boat began to move in his direction, and he was about to dive below the water to elude observation when he saw a huge black mass rolling onwards towards him.

It was a tintorea, a shark of the most voracious kind.

Although the Indian dived immediately, he was soon obliged to come to the surface to take breath. As he rose he was struck by the tail of the shark, and felt the slimy scales against his breast. In order to grasp its prey, the animal, according to its habit, rolled over on its back, and displayed its monstrous jaw armed with its triple rows of teeth; but in an instant, Martin, catching a glimpse of its white belly, made a desperate effort, and plunged in his dagger to its very hilt.

The waves around him were all red with blood; he made another dive, and, rising about ten fathoms away, had entirely lost sight of the boat. A few more strokes, and he regained the shore, hardly conscious of the hairbreadth escape he had had from the most terrible of deaths.

Next day he was gone from Chorillos, and Don Vegal, harassed by misgivings, hurried with all speed to Lima, in the hope of finding him.

CHAPTER VII
THE BRIDE DISAPPEARS

QUITE an event was the approaching marriage of André Certa with the daughter of the affluent Jew. The ladies had no time for repose; the necessity of inventing new fashions and for preparing elaborate costumes to grace the occasion occupied every thought and taxed every resource.

The mansion of the Jew was especially the scene of bustle, as he was resolved to give a most sumptuous entertainment in honor of Sarah's wedding. The frescoes which decorated the walls in Spanish fashion were restored at a large expense; hangings of the most costly quality were hung at every window and over every door; handsome furniture, carved of fragrant wood, diffused a pleasant odor throughout the spacious rooms, while plants of the rarest and loveliest growth, the products of the most luxuriant regions of the tropics, adorned the balconies and terraces at every turn.

The maiden herself, however, was the victim of despair. Sambo had no longer any hope, otherwise he would have worn the red token on his arm. Her servant Liberta had been sent to keep a watch upon the old Indian, but he had been unable to discover anything.

Could the girl only have been free to follow the dictates of her heart she would not have hesitated an instant to have sought a refuge in the nearest convent, and to have made her vows for all her future life. Attracted as she was with the doctrines of the Catholics as they had been irresistibly expounded to her by the eloquence of Father Joachim, she would have surrendered herself with the most genuine of zeal to the influences of that faith which was winding itself so sympathetically around the longings of her heart.

The monk, anxious to avoid every suspicion of scandal, and being better read in his breviary than in the passions of human nature, allowed Sarah to believe in the death of Martin Paz. The girl's conversion seemed to him the matter of supreme importance, and presuming that this would be secured by her marriage with André, he tried to reconcile her to the union, without at all knowing the conditions under which it was concluded.

At length the day arrived, a day so full of congratulations to one party, so heavy in misgivings to the other. André Certa had issued his invitation to well-nigh the whole town, but had the mortification of finding that, under some pretext or other, all the superior families had excused themselves.

The hour struck at which the marriage contract had to be signed, and expectation rose to its height, when all became aware that the bride had not appeared.

The annoyance and alarm of the old Jew were intense. The frown that lowered on the brow of André Certa was the witness of mingled anger and amazement. Embarrassment seized every guest; and the whole scene was brought out in singular distinctness by the thousands of wax lights, whose rays were reflected from the countless mirrors.

Meanwhile, outside in the general thoroughfare, there was a man pacing up and down in a state of the wildest excitement. That man was the Marquis Don Vegal.

CHAPTER VIII
THE RESCUE

THROUGHOUT this period Sarah, a prey to the bitterest anguish, remained in the solitude of her own room. Nothing could induce her to quit it. Once, half stifled by her emotion, she sought relief by going to the balcony that overhung the garden below.

At that very instant she caught sight of a man wending his way through the groves of magnolias, and recognized her servant Liberta. To all appearance he was stealthily watching someone who did not see him. At one moment he was concealing himself behind a statue, at the next he was crouching on the grass.

Then all at once the girl turned pale. There was Liberta struggling with a tall man who had thrown him to the ground, and who was pressing his hand over his mouth so that he could only utter a feeble groan. She was about to cry out, when she saw the two men rise together from the ground, and deliberately make a survey of each other.

"You! you! is it you?" said Liberta.

There had risen to her vision what appeared to be a phantom from another world, and as Liberta now followed the man who had felled him to the earth, she recognized Martin Paz, and was unable to do more than re-echo the words she had heard, "You! you! is it you?"

Gazing at her intently, Martin addressed her with an earnest appeal.

"Does the bride hear the revelry of the bridal feast? Are not the guests speeding to the hall, that they may rejoice in the beauty of her charms? The victim, is she prepared for the sacrifice? Is it with these pale cheeks, and trembling lips, that she is going to surrender herself to the bridegroom?"

She scarcely understood him, but he continued his pathetic address, "Why should the maiden weep? There is peace *there;* far away from the house of her father; far away from the home where she drops her tears of bitterness; there is peace *there.*"

And drawing himself to his full height, he stood pointing with his finger to the summits of the Cordilleras, as if showing that there was a refuge in the mountains to which she might escape.

The girl felt herself constrained by an irresistible impulse. There were voices close to her very chamber; she heard the sound of approaching footsteps; her father was on his way, perchance the man to whom she was betrothed was coming too. Suddenly Martin Paz extinguished the lamp that hung above her head, and his whistle, just as on that evening on the Plaza-Mayor, resounded shrilly through the gathering shades of night.

The door burst open. Samuel and André Certa hurried in. The darkness was all bewildering. The servants hastened to bring some lanterns; but the room was empty.

"Death and fury!" shrieked the half-breed.

"Where is she?" exclaimed the Jew.

"For this," said André, with the coarsest insolence, "I hold you responsible."

A cold sweat came over the old man, and uttering a cry of anguish, he rushed away, followed by his servants.

All this time Martin Paz had been flying, at fullest speed, along the streets of the town. Summoned by his well-known signal, at about two hundred paces from Samuel's house, there were several Indians ready at his call.

"Away to our mountains!" he cried.

"To the Marquis Don Vegal's!" came from a voice close behind. The Indian turned, and found the marquis standing by his side.

"Will you not trust the maiden to me?" said Don Vegal.

Martin bowed his head in token of assent, and said in a smothered voice: "To the house of Don Vegal!"

Thus yielding her to the marquis, Martin had every confidence that the girl would be in safety, and from a feeling of what was owing to propriety, he resolved that he would not himself pass the night under the marquis's roof.

He made his way in another direction; his head was hot, and a fevered blood was throbbing in his veins; but he had hardly gone a hundred yards, when a party of half a dozen men threw themselves across his path, and in spite of his obstinate resistance, secured his arms, and blindfolded him. He raised a cry of desperation, supposing that he had fallen into the hands of his foes.

It did not take many minutes to convey him to a neighboring resort, and on the bandage being removed from his eyes, he saw that he was in a low room of the tavern where his associates had organized their scheme of revolution.

Sambo, who had been present at the rescue of the young girl, was there; Manangani and some others were standing round him. Martin's eyes flashed angrily.

"No pity had my son for me," said Sambo. "Shame that for so long he should permit me to believe that he was dead."

"Is it fair," asked Manangani, "that on the very eve of a revolution, Martin Paz, our chief, should betake himself to the quarters of the enemy."

Not a word fell from the lips of the prisoner in reply to either one or the other.

"Why should it be tolerated," demanded Manangani, "that our interests should be sacrificed to a woman?" and as he spoke he approached nearer to Martin, holding a poignard in his hand. Martin Paz did not even glance at him, but still stood perfectly unmoved.

"Let us speak first," said Sambo, "and act afterwards. If my son is disloyal to his brethren, I shall know how to exact a proper vengeance. Let him be on his guard! That Jew's daughter is not concealed so closely as to elude our grasp. He must think betimes. Let him once be condemned to die, and there will not be a stone in the town on which he could rest his head; let him, on the other hand, be the deliverer of his country, and he may crown that head with perpetual glory!"

Although Martin Paz did not break his silence, it was obvious that a mighty struggle was going on within his soul: Sambo had succeeded in stirring the depths of that ardent nature.

For all the projects of insurrection Martin Paz was indispensable. His was an influence over the Indians of the town which none but himself enjoyed; he bent them at his will; he had but to give the word, and they were prepared to follow him to death.

By Sambo's order the bonds were removed from his arms, and he stood at liberty. The old Indian looked at him steadily, and bade him once more listen. "To-morrow," he said, "is the feast of the Amanacäes. While the festival is at its height, our brethren will fall like an avalanche upon the unarmed and unsuspecting men of Lima. Now take your choice. There is the way to the mountains: there is the way to the town. You are free!"

"To the mountains! to the mountains!" shouted Martin; "and death to our foes!"

And the first rays of the rising sun cast a ruddy glow into the council-chamber of the Indian chiefs in the heart of the Cordilleras.

CHAPTER IX
THE FESTIVAL

AND now the great annual fête of the Amanacäes had arrived. It was the 24th of June. On foot, on horseback, in carriages, the bulk of the population made its way to the well-known spot about half a league from the town. Indians and half-breeds were wont alike to share the mutual recreation; kinsmen and acquaintances marched gayly to the festive scene. Each group carried its own stock of provisions, and many of them were headed by a musician, who accompanied the popular melodies which he sung with the notes of his guitar. Starting through the fields of maize and indigo, they entered the banana-groves beyond, and traversed the charming avenues of willows which led them to the woods, where the aromatic odor of citrons and oranges mingled with the wild perfume of the hills. All along the route the itinerant vendors hawked a liberal supply of beer and brandy, which served to excite the merriment, and at times to stimulate the boisterousness of the pleasure-seeking multitude. Equestrians made their horses prance in the very middle of the crowd, vying with one another in displaying their speed and dexterity.

The festival derives its name from the little flowers that grow on the mountains. There is a universal license, yet it is exceedingly rare for the noise of a quarrel to be heard mingling with the thousand demonstrations of general joy. A few lancers here and there, wearing their flashing cuirasses, are more than sufficient to preserve order among the teeming crowds.

But whilst the festive crowd was enjoying the fair prospect, a bloody tragedy had been prepared below the snowy summits of the Cordilleras. Whilst the homes of Lima were being deserted by their occupants, a great number of Indians were wandering about the streets. They had been usually accustomed to join the general festivity, but on this occasion they went to and fro in the town, silent and preoccupied. Every now and then a busy chief would give them some secret order, and pass quickly on his way. Little by little they concentrated all their force upon the richest quarters of the town.

Thus the day of rejoicing passed on, and as the sun began to sink into the west, the time arrived in which the aristocrats in their turn went out to join the general throng. The costliest of dresses were seen in the handsomest of carriages which lined the avenues on either side of the road that led to the Amancäes, and pedestrians, horses, and vehicles were mingled in inextricable confusion.

The cathedral clock now tolled the hour of five.

Up from the town there rose a mighty cry. At a concerted signal, masses of armed Indians from many a byway and many a house, rushed out and filled the streets. The wealthiest districts were almost in a moment invaded by troops of the revolutionary tribe, not a few of whom were brandishing lighted torches high above their heads.

"Death to the Spaniards! Death and destruction to the tyrants!" were the watch-words of the rebels. Forthwith from the surrounding heights came trooping in a multitude of other Indians, hurrying to aid their brethren in the general uproar.

Imagination can scarcely realize the alarming aspect of the town at this moment. The revolutionists had penetrated in all directions. At the head of one party, Martin Paz was waving a black flag, and whilst some detachments were assaulting the houses that were doomed to pillage, he led his troops towards the Plaza-Mayor. Close beside him was the ferocious Manangani, bellowing out his infuriated orders.

But forewarned of the revolt, the soldiers of the Government had ranged themselves in a line along the front of the president's palace, and a general fusillade startled the insurgents as they approached. Taken thoroughly by surprise at this reception, and seeing many of their number fall, the Indians, frantic with excitement, made a tremendous rush upon the troops, and great was the *mêlée* that ensued. Both Martin Paz and Manangani performed prodigies of valor, and it was only marvelous how they escaped with their lives. It was of all things most essential that the palace should be taken, and that they should establish themselves within its walls.

"Forward!" cried Martin Paz, as again and again he urged his followers to the assault.

Although they had been routed in many quarters, the besiegers nevertheless succeeded in causing the battalion of soldiers that guarded the front of the palace to beat a retreat, and Manangani had already placed his foot upon the flight of steps when he was brought to a sudden stand. The reserve troops behind had unmasked two pieces of artillery, and were preparing to open fire.

There was not a moment to lose; the battery must be captured before it could be brought into action.

"We two must do it," shouted Manangani vehemently.

But Martin did not hear him; he was attending to a negro, who was whispering in his ear that the house of the Marquis Don Vegal was being plundered, and that there was every chance that the marquis himself would be assassinated.

Martin Paz began to retreat. To no purpose did Manangani rally him to the attack, and all at once the roar of the cannon was heard, and the Indians were swept down on every side.

"Follow me!" shouted Martin, and gathering a handful of companions around him, he succeeded in effecting a passage back through the line of soldiers.

It was a retreat that had all the evil consequences of an act of treachery. The Indians believed themselves abandoned by their chief, and in vain did Manangani urge them to renew the fight. A heavy fusillade threw them into utter disorder, and their rout was soon complete. Flames at a little distance attracted some of the fugitives to the work of pillage, but the soldiers pursued them with their swords, and killed them in considerable numbers.

Meanwhile Martin Paz had reached the residence of Don Vegal, and found it the scene of a furious struggle. Sambo was there taking the lead in the work of destruction. He had a double motive to urge him on; not only was he eager to plunder the Spaniard, but he was anxious to get possession of Sarah as a pledge of his son's fidelity.

The gate and the walls of the great courtyard were thrown down, and revealed the marquis, sword in hand, supported by his servants, and making a vigorous defence against the mob that was assailing him. His determined attitude and indomitable courage gave a certain sublimity to his appearance; he stood foremost in the fray, and his own arm had laid low the corpses that were on the ground before him.

But altogether hopeless seemed the struggle he was making against the numbers of Indians, which were now recruited by the arrival of those who had been vanquished on the Plaza-Mayor. He was all but succumbing to the superior force of his opponents, when, like a thunderbolt, Martin Paz fell upon the insurgents in the rear, compelling them to face about, and then making his way through a shower of bullets to the marquis's side, he protected him with his own body from the blows which assailed him.

"Well done! well done! my friend!" shouted Don Vegal, clasping his defender's hand.

"Well done! well done! Martin Paz," repeated another voice that went to his very soul.

He recognized Sarah; her words gave redoubled vigor to his arm, and a veritable circle of bleeding figures lay stretched around him.

Sambo's troops meanwhile were forced to yield. Twenty times did the modern Brutus make his unsuccessful assaults upon his son, and twenty times did Martin Paz withhold his hand, which was able, if he would, to strike down his father.

Covered with blood, Manangani suddenly took his stand at Sambo's side, and spurred him on to vengeance. "Your oath!" he cried. "Remember your oath! You have sworn to avenge the traitor's guilt upon his kinsman, upon his friends, upon himself! The time has come! See, here are the soldiers, and André Certa is with them!"

"Come on, then," said Sambo, with the laugh of a maniac; "come on now!"

Then leaving the courtyard, the two together made their way towards a body of troops who were hastening to the scene; they were aimed at by the advancing corps, but not in the least intimidated, Sambo made his way straight up to André Certa.

"You are André Certa," he said. "Your bride is in Don Vegal's house, and Martin Paz is going to carry her off to yonder mountains."

He said no more, and both the Indians disappeared. In this way Sambo had prevailed to bring the two mortal antagonists face to face. The soldiers were misled by the presence of Martin Paz, and rushed onwards to attack the house.

Maddened with fury was André Certa. As soon as he caught sight of Martin he made a dash upon him. The young Indian, as he recognized the half-breed, howled out a challenge of defiance, and quitted the flight of steps which he had so valiantly defended.

Here then stood the rivals: foot to foot, breast to breast, face to face. Keen was the survey that each took of the other. Neither friend nor enemy ventured to approach; all alike looked on in terror, and with bated breath. André first made a desperate lunge at Martin Paz, who had dropped his dagger; but, just in time to escape the blow, Martin had grasped André's uplifted arm. André tried in vain to disengage it, and Martin, wresting the poignard from his adversary's hand, plunged it into his very heart.

Martin threw himself into the arms of the marquis, who shouted impetuously, " Now quick, off, off to the mountains; wait no further bidding, but fly!"

At this instant old Samuel made his appearance, and flinging himself upon Certa's body, drew out a small pocketbook which the dead man had upon him. The action did not however escape the observation of Martin, who, turning upon the Jew, snatched the book from his hands, and turning over the leaves, extracted a paper, which, with an exclamation of joy, he handed to the marquis.

The marquis looked confounded as he slowly read the words, " Received of Señor André Certa the sum of 100,000 piastres: which I undertake to restore, if Sarah, whom I saved from the wreck of the *San José*, should not prove to be the daughter and sole heiress of the Marquis Don Vegal."

" Daughter! my daughter!" exclaimed the bewildered Spaniard, and hurried towards the apartment where Sarah was concealed.

The girl had gone. Father Joachim was there, covered in blood, and could only utter a few disjointed words, " Sambo . . . carried off . . . Rio Madeira!"

CHAPTER X
UNITED IN DEATH

" OFF," said Martin Paz, " let us be off!"

And without saying a word, the marquis quickly followed the Indian's lead. His daughter! Yes, at all hazards he must find his daughter.

Mules were brought without delay, and the two men mounted. They had buckled on large gaiters below their knees, and put on broad-brimmed straw hats to shade their heads; they carried pistols in their holsters, and their rifles were slung to their sides. Martin had fastened his lasso around him, attaching one end to the harness of his mule.

Well enough did he know every plain and every pass of that mountain-chain, and had no doubt as to the district into which Sambo would attempt to convey the maiden; his betrothed he longed to call her; but did he dare thus to think of Don Vegal's daughter?

One thought, one aim, occupied alike the Indian and the Spaniard, as they penetrated the gorges of the Cordilleras, darkened by the plantations of pines and cocoa-trees. They had left behind the cedars, the cotton-trees, and the aloes; they had passed beyond the fields planted with luzerne and maize. To traverse the mountains at this season was a perilous undertaking. The melting of the snow beneath the rays of the summer sun had swollen the streams to cataracts, and continually immense masses came rolling down from the peaks above into the chasms below.

But neither by day nor night did the father and the lover permit themselves to rest. They had reached the point, the very highest in the chain, and, worn out with fatigue, seemed ready to fall into that condition of despair which deprives men of all power to act. It required almost a superhuman effort to go on; but turning to the eastern declivity of the mountain-range, they fell upon traces of the fugitives, and with rekindled energy began the descent.

Reaching the almost boundless virgin forests that cover the regions between Brazil and Peru, they made their way through woods that might have proved inextricable had not the practiced sagacity of Martin stood them in good stead. Nothing escaped his observation; and the ashes of an extinguished fire, some vestiges of footsteps, some twigs broken off from the branches, and the character of certain fragments in the path—all attracted his experienced eye.

Don Vegal feared that his ill-fated daughter had been conveyed on foot over the crags and through the thickets, but the Indian pointed out to him some indications in the stony ground which were undoubtedly the impressions of an animal's feet; and, above all, the branches had been broken back in the same direction, and that at a height which could only be reached by a person that was mounted. The marquis too gladly yielded his conviction, and rejoiced to think that for Martin Paz there was no obstacle insurmountable, and no peril that he could not overcome.

At length one evening, postively worn out by fatigue, they made a halt. They had just come to the banks of a river. It was the upper stream of the Madeira, which the Indian knew perfectly well. Enormous mangroves overhung the water and connected themselves with the trees on the farther bank by creepers hanging in fanciful festoons. The question at once arose about the fugitives. Had they gone up the stream, or followed it farther down? or had they contrived by any means to go straight across? It was all important to decide, and Martin took unbounded pains to follow up some footprints for a distance along the rocks till he came to a glade which was somewhat less dense than the surrounding woods. There he observed such indentations in the soil, as left him no doubt that a group of people had crossed the river at that very spot.

" To-morrow," he said, " perhaps our journey may be over."

" Nay, let us go on now," said the marquis.

" We must cross the river," replied Martin.

" Well, why not swim across at once? "

And without delay they proceeded to undress, and tying up their clothes in a bundle, that Martin proposed to carry over on his head, they made their way into the stream as noiselessly as possible, that they might not disturb any of the alligators that are abundant in all the rivers both of Peru and Brazil.

On arriving safely at the farther bank Martin Paz made it his first care to search for the track which the Indians must have made, but after a long search amidst the fallen leaves, and along the pebbly shore, he was able to discover nothing. Remembering, however, that the strength of the current had very probably made them drift away from a straight course, they reascended the bank for a considerable distance, when they came upon footprints so decided that they could not be mistaken.

It was manifestly the place where Sambo had effected his passage over the Madeira with his troop, which had been largely increased on its way. The truth was that the Indians of the mountains and the plains, who had been impatiently expecting the success of their insurrection, now learned that it had miscarried through treachery; burning with rage, and finding that there was a victim on whom to vent their wrath, they had joined themselves to the old Indian's retinue.

The young girl had little consciousness of what was going on around her. She went forwards because there were hands that urged her forwards.. Had they left her in the middle of the wilderness she would not have stirred a step to escape death. The memory of the young Indian would now and then flit across her mind, yet she was little otherwise than an inanimate burden upon the neck of the mule that carried her. Beyond the river, when two of the men dragged her along on foot, she left a trace of blood, marking every spot on which she trod.

It did not occur to Sambo, and therefore gave him no uneasiness, that the dotted crimson streak was an index to point out the way they went. He was approaching the limit of his flight, and soon the rushing cataracts of the river were heard with their deafening roar.

The party halted at an insignificant village, comprising about a hundred huts, made of canes and clay. As they entered, a multitude of women and children greeted them with boisterous acclamations; but all their delight was changed to rage as soon as they heard of the supposed treachery of Martin Paz.

Without quailing in any way before her enemies, Sarah surveyed them with a languid gaze. Though they insulted her with the vilest gestures, and assailed her ears with obloquy and savage threats, she was passive and unmoved.

"Where is my husband?" demanded one of the angry crones; "he has been killed through you."

"My brother too," added another, "he has not come back again; my brother has lost his life for you!"

Then the general chorus rose aloud, "Die! you shall die! and your flesh shall be given piecemeal to us all!"

And as they shouted, they brandished their knives aloft, waved torches of burning fire, took up stones of prodigious weight, and heaped repeated menaces on her head.

"Stop!" cried Sambo, "let us hear the judgment of the chiefs!"

In obedience to his order they stayed their demonstrations of revenge, and contented themselves with casting angry glances at the girl, who had sunk down for rest, bespattered as she was with blood, upon the stony margin of the stream.

Just below the village, the Rio Madeira, after being pent up between narrow confines, made its escape in a roaring cataract, which precipitated itself in a mighty volume to a depth of more than a hundred feet. The sentence passed on Sarah was that she should be cast into the flood immediately above the point from which the rapid made its start. At the first dawn of morning she was to be tied to a canoe of bark, and left to the mercy of the current of the Madeira.

That the execution of the sentence was deferred till the morrow, was not for the purpose of giving respite to the condemned victim, but only that she might be reserved for a night of terror and alarm.

The publication of the verdict was a signal for universal joy, and a frantic outburst of delight spread all around.

The night was spent in the wildest orgies. The Indians became intoxicated with their draughts of burning brandy; they danced in derisive revelry around the passive girl; they rushed about with disheveled hair, and scoured the wilderness around, waving aloft great flaming pine-branches. Thus they continued till the early twilight of the morning; and thus, with yet frantic frenzy, they saluted the first rays of the rising sun.

The fatal hour arrived, and no sooner was the girl liberated from the stake to which she had been secured, than a hundred arms were voluntarily outstretched to bear her to the scene of punishment. The name of Martin Paz escaped her lips, and the outcry of hatred and revenge waxed louder than before. In order to reach the highest level of the stream, they had to clamber by the roughest paths up the rocks that overhung the bed of the river, so that when she arrived Sarah was besprinkled once again with blood. They found the bark canoe in readiness at about a hundred yards above the waterfall, and having laid their prisoner down they lashed her in her place with cords that cut deeply into her very flesh.

The cry of the multitude went up as the cry of one man— " Vengeance! "

Whirling round and round, the canoe was carried rapidly along. At this moment, upon the opposite bank, were seen two men, Martin Paz and Don Vegal.

" My daughter! my daughter! " shouted the father as he fell upon his knees.

The canoe swept onwards nearer to the fall. Mounted upon a rock, Martin Paz unwound his long lasso, which whistled round his head, and at the very instant when the canoe was being sucked into the eddy of the cataract, the long leather lash was uncoiled, and caught the canoe in its sliding noose.

"Death and destruction!" howled the horde of Indians, beside themselves with rage.

Martin Paz raised his tall figure to its fullest height, and gently drew the canoe, which had been hovering over the abyss, nearer and nearer to himself.

Suddenly an arrow came whizzing through the air, and Martin Paz, falling forwards into the frail bark that carried Sarah, was swallowed up with her in the whirlpool of the cataract. Within a moment another arrow had pierced Don Vegal's heart.

It was bliss to Sarah to know that she and Martin Paz were joined in eternal nuptials, and the last thought of the maiden was that he was thus baptized into the faith which in her heart she loved.

THE END

The Mutineers
OR
A Tragedy of Mexico

The Mutineers

CHAPTER I
FROM GUAJAN TO ACAPULCO

O N the 18th of October, 1825, the *Asia,* a high-built Spanish ship, and the *Constanzia,* a brig of eighteen guns, cast anchor off the island of Guajan, one of the Mariannas. The crews of these vessels, badly-fed, ill-paid, and harassed with fatigue during the six months occupied by their passage from Spain, had been secretly plotting a mutiny.

The spirit of insubordination more especially exhibited itself on board the *Constanzia,* commanded by Captain Don Orteva, a man of iron will, whom nothing could bend. The brig had been impeded in her progress by several serious accidents, so unforeseen that they could alone, it was evident, have been caused by intentional malice. The *Asia,* commanded by Don Roque de Guzuarte, had been compelled consequently to put into port with her. One night the compass was broken, no one knew how; on another the shrouds of the foremast gave way as if they had been cut, and the mast with all its rigging fell over the side. Lastly, during important maneuvers, on two occasions the rudder-ropes broke in the most unaccountable manner.

Don Orteva had especially to keep an eye on two men of his crew—his lieutenant Martinez and José the captain of the maintop. Lieutenant Martinez, who had already compromised his character as an officer by joining in the cabals of the forecastle, had in consequence been several times under arrest, and during his imprisonment, the midshipman Pablo had done duty as lieutenant of the *Constanzia.*

Young Pablo was one of those gallant natures whose generosity prompts them to dare anything. He was an orphan who, saved and brought up by Captain Orteva, would readily have given his life for that of his benefactor.

The evening before they were to leave Guajan, Lieutenant Martinez went to a low tavern, where he met several petty officers, and seamen of both ships.

"Comrades!" exclaimed Martinez, "thanks to the accidents which so opportunely happened, the ship and the brig were compelled to put into port, and I have been enabled to come here that I might discuss secretly with you some important matters!"

"Bravo!" replied the party of men, with one voice.

"Speak, lieutenant," exclaimed several of the sailors, "and let us hear your plans."

"This is my scheme," answered Martinez. "As soon as we shall have made ourselves masters of the two vessels, we will steer a course for the coast of Mexico. You must know that the new Confederation possesses no ships of war; she will, therefore, be eager to buy our ships without asking questions, and not only shall we regularly receive our pay for the future, but the price we obtain for the ships will be fairly divided among us."

"Agreed!"

"And what shall be the signal for acting in concert on board the two ships?" asked José the topman.

"A rocket fired from the *Asia*," answered Martinez; "that shall be the moment for action. We are ten to one, and the officers of the ship and the brig will be made prisoners before they will have time to know what is happening."

"When shall we look out for the signal?" asked one of the boatswain's mates of the *Constanzia*.

"In a few days hence, when we shall be off the island of Mindanao."

"But the Mexicans, will they not receive our ships with cannon shots?" inquired José in a hesitating tone. "If I mistake not, the Confederation has issued a decree to prohibit any Spanish ships from entering her harbors, and instead of gold it will be iron and lead they will be sending on board us!"

"Don't trouble yourself about that, José. We will let them know who we are from a distance," answered Martinez.

"How is that to be done?"

"By hoisting the Mexican colors at the gaffs of our ships;" and saying this, Lieutenant Martinez displayed before the eyes of the mutineers, a green, white, and red flag.

The exhibition of this emblem of Mexican independence was rceived with gloomy silence.

"Do you already regret the flag of Spain?" cried the lieutenant in a mocking tone. "Very well, let those who feel such regrets at once separate from us, and pleasantly continue the voyage under the orders of Captain Don Roque, or Commander Don Orteva. As for us, who do not wish any longer to obey them, we shall soon find the means of rendering them helpless."

"We'll stick by you," cried the whole party with one accord.

During this time Don Orteva was sadly troubled with sinister forebodings. He was well aware how completely fallen was the Spanish navy; that insubordination had greatly contributed to its destruction. On the other hand his patriotism would not allow him to reflect calmly on the successive reverses which had overtaken his country, to which, as it seemed to him, the revolt of the Mexican States had put the finishing stroke. He was frequently in the habit of conversing with the midshipman Pablo on these serious matters, and he especially took a satisfaction in talking to him of the former supremacy of the Spanish navy in every part of the ocean.

"My boy," said he one day, "we have no longer discipline among our sailors. There are, especially, signs of mutiny on board this vessel; and it is possible—indeed I have a foreboding—that some abominable treason will deprive me of life! But you will avenge me, will you not? You will at the same time avenge Spain; for will not the blow which strikes me, be really aimed at her?"

"I swear it, Captain Orteva!" answered Pablo.

"Do not make yourself the enemy of anyone on board the brig, but remember when the day comes, my boy—that unhappy time—the best mode of serving one's country is first to watch, and then to chastise, the wretched beings who would betray her."

"I promise you that I will die!" answered the midshipman, "yes, that I will die, should it be necessary, to punish the traitors!"

Pablo went below. Martinez remained alone on the poop and turned his eyes toward the *Asia,* which was sailing to leeward of the brig. The evening was magnificent, and presaged one of those lovely nights in the tropics which are both fresh and calm.

The lieutenant endeavored to ascertain in the gloom who were the men on watch. He recognized José and those sailors with whom he had held the meeting at the island of Guajan. Martinez immediately approached the man at the helm. He spoke two words to him in a low voice, and that was all. But it might have been observed that the helm was put a little more a-weather than before, so that the brig sensibly drew nearer the larger ship.

Contrary to the usual custom on board ship, Martinez paced up and down on the lee side, in order that he might obtain an uninterrupted view of the *Asia*. Restless and agitated, he kept turning a speaking-trumpet round and round in his hand.

Suddenly a report was heard on board the ship.

At this signal Martinez leaped on to the hammock-nettings, and in a loud voice, " All hands on deck ! " he cried. " Brail up the courses ! "

At that moment Don Orteva, followed by his officers, came out of his cabin, and addressing himself to the lieutenant, " Why was that order given ? "

At this moment some fresh reports were heard from on board the *Asia*.

Don Orteva, turning to the few men who remained near him, " Stand by me, my brave lads ! " he cried. And advancing towards Martinez, " Seize that officer ! " he exclaimed.

" Death to the commander ! " replied Martinez.

Pablo and two officers drew their swords and held their pistols in their hands. Some seamen, led by the honest boatswain Jacopo, were rushing to their support, but, quickly stopped by the mutineers, were disarmed and rendered incapable of giving assistance.

The marines and the crew, drawn up across the entire width of the deck, advanced towards their officers. The men who had remained staunch to their duty, driven into a corner of the poop, had but one course to take—it was to throw themselves on the mutineers. Don Orteva pointed the muzzle of his pistol at Martinez.

At that moment a rocket was seen to rise from the deck of the *Asia*.

" Our friends have succeeded ! " cried Martinez.

The bullet from Don Orteva's pistol was lost in space. The captain crossed swords with the lieutenant, but, overwhelmed by numbers and severely wounded, he was borne to the deck. His officers in a few seconds shared his fate.

Blue lights were now let off in the rigging of the brig, and replied to by others from the *Asia*. The mutiny had at the same moment broken out and proved triumphant on board the ship. Lieutenant Martinez was master of the *Constanzia*, and his prisoners were thrust pell mell into the main cabin.

"To the yard-arm with them!" shouted several of the most savage.

"Trice them up, trice them up! Dead men tell no tales!"

Lieutenant Martinez, at the head of these bloodthirsty mutineers, was rushing towards the main cabin, but the rest of the crew strongly objected to so cruel a massacre, and the officers were saved.

"Bring Don Orteva up on deck," cried Martinez.

His orders were obeyed; and the captain was bound to the rail of the brig, concealed by the mainsail. While there he was heard to shout out to his lieutenant, "Oh, you scoundrel! You base traitor!"

Martinez, losing all control over himself, leaped on the poop with an axe in his hand. Being prevented from reaching the captain, with a single vigorous stroke he cut the main sheet. The main boom, forced violently by the wind, struck the hapless Don Orteva on the head, and he fell lifeless on the deck.

A cry of horror rose from the crew of the brig.

"His death was accidental!" exclaimed Lieutenant Martinez. "Heave the body overboard!"

The two vessels, keeping close together, ran towards the coast of Mexico. The next morning an island was seen abeam. The boats of the *Asia* and *Constanzia* were lowered, and the officers, with the exception of the midshipman Pablo and Jacopo the boatswain, who had both submitted to Martinez, were landed on its desert shore. But a few days subsequently they were all happily taken off by an English whaler and conveyed to Manila.

Some weeks after the events which have been described, the two vessels anchored in the Bay of Monterey, on the coast of Old California. Martinez, going on shore, informed the military governor of the port of his intentions. He offered to carry to Mexico the two Spanish vessels with their stores and guns, and to place their crews at the command of the Confederation. In return, all he asked was that the Mexican government should pay the whole of the wages due to them since they quitted Spain.

In reply to these overtures, the governor said that he had not sufficient authority to treat with him. He recommended Martinez to sail for Mexico, where he could himself easily settle the matter. The lieutenant followed this advice, and leaving the *Asia* at Monterey, after a month devoted to pleasure on shore, he again sailed in the *Constanzia*. Pablo, Jacopo, and José formed part of the crew of the brig, which with a fair wind under all sail, made the best of her way for the port of Acapulco.

CHAPTER II
FROM ACAPULCO TO CIGUALAN

OF the four ports which Mexico possesses on the side of the Pacific Ocean, namely, San Blas, Zacatula, Tehuantepec, and Acapulco, the last offers the greatest accommodation to shipping. The town, it is true, is badly built and unhealthy, but the anchorage is secure, and the harbor can easily contain a hundred vessels. Lofty cliffs shelter the ships at anchor from every wind, and form so tranquil a basin, that a stranger arriving by land looks down upon what he may suppose to be a lake surrounded by mountains.

Acapulco was at this time protected by three forts flanking it on the right side, while the entrance was defended by a battery of seven guns which could, when necessary, cross their fire at a right angle with those of Fort San Diego. That fort, armed with thirty pieces of artillery, completely commanded the harbor, and would inevitably have sent to the bottom any craft which might have attempted to force an entrance into the port.

The town had therefore nothing to fear, notwithstanding which, a universal panic seized the inhabitants three months after the events which have just been related.

It happened thus: A ship was signaled approaching the port. So completely did the people of Acapulco doubt the intentions of the stranger, that nothing would make them believe that she came as a friend. That which the new

Confederation mostly feared, and not without reason, was to be again brought under the dominion of Spain. This was because, notwithstanding that a treaty of commerce had been signed with Great Britain, and a *chargé d'affaires* had arrived from London, which court had acknowledged the Republic, the Mexican Government did not possess a single ship to protect their coast. However that might be, the strange vessel was evidently some hardy adventurer, which the northwesterly gales, blustering on their shores from the autumnal equinox to the spring, had probably driven hither with shivered canvas.

If this was not the case, the people of Acapulco could not tell what to think, and at all events they were making every possible preparation to resist the expected attack of the stranger, when the suspicious vessel ran up to her peak the flag of Mexican independence!

Having got to about half cannon-shot from the port, the *Constanzia,* whose name could be clearly read on her counter, suddenly came to an anchor, her sails were furled, and a boat, which was at once lowered, pulled rapidly towards the harbor.

Lieutenant Martinez, having disembarked from her, proceeded at once to the governor, to whom he explained the circumstances which brought him to the place. The latter highly approved of the resolution taken by the lieutenant to join the Mexicans, and assured him that General Guadalupe, President of the Confederation, would certainly agree to purchase the two vessels.

No sooner was the news known in the town than the people broke out into transports of joy. The whole population turned out to admire the first vessel of the Mexican navy, and saw in their new possession, with this proof of the disorganization prevailing in the Spanish service, the means of more completely defeating all fresh attempts which might be made by their former and much hated oppressors to overcome them.

Martinez returned on board the brig. Some hours afterwards the *Constanzia* was anchored in the port, and her crew were quartered among the inhabitants of Acapulco. When, however, Martinez called over the roll of his followers, neither Pablo nor Jacopo answered to their names. They had both disappeared!

The following day two horsemen set out from Acapulco on the deserted and mountainous road for Mexico City. The horsemen were Martinez and José. The sailor was well acquainted with the road. He had on numerous occasions climbed these mountains of Anahuac. So well did he know it, that although an Indian guide had offered his services they had been declined.

"Let us ride faster!" said Martinez, sticking his spurs into his horse's flanks. "I have my doubts about this disappearance of Pablo and Jacopo. Can they mean to make the bargain for themselves, and rob us of our shares?"

"By St. Jago! they won't be very far wrong there," sulkily repiled the seaman. "It will be a case of thieves robbing thieves, such as we are."

"How many days will it take us to reach Mexico?"

"Four or five, lieutenant—a mere walk; but not so fast; you surely see what a steep hill there is before us."

In reality they had reached the first slopes which form the sides of the mountains rising above the wide plains.

"Our horses are not shod," said the seaman, pulling up, "and their hoofs will soon be worn out on these granite rocks."

"Let us push on," exclaimed Martinez, setting the example. "Our horses come from the farms of Southern Mexico, and in their journeys across the Savannahs they are unaccustomed to these inequalities in the ground. Let us profit therefore by the evenness of the road, and make the best of our way out of these vast solitudes, which are not formed to put us in good spirits."

"Does Lieutenant Martinez feel any remorse?" asked José, shrugging his shoulders.

"Remorse! No."

Martinez fell back into perfect silence, and the two travelers made their steeds move on at a rapid trot.. The sun had sunk beneath the horizon when they reached the village of Cigualan. The village is composed of a few huts inhabited by poor Indians, who are generally known as tame Indians—that is to say, they cultivate the soil.

The two Spaniards were received with but scant hospitality. The Indians recognized them as belonging to the nation of their ancient oppressors, and showed themselves but little inclined to render them assistance. This was in consequence of the fact, that two other travelers had a short time before passed through the village, and had laid violent hands on the small amount of available food which they could discover. The lieutenant and his comrade paid no attention to these circumstances, which indeed appeared to them nothing extraordinary.

In a short time they secured food, and dined, as men do after a long journey, with sharp appetites. The repast finished, they stretched themselves on the ground with their daggers in their hands; they then, notwithstanding the hardness of their couches, and the incessant biting of the mosquitos, overcome by fatigue, quickly fell asleep.

During the night Martinez frequently started up and, in an agitated voice, repeated the names of Jacopo and Pablo, whose disappearance so completely occupied his mind.

CHAPTER III
FROM CIGUALAN TO CUERNAVACA

THE next morning at daybreak, the horses were saddled and bridled. The travelers, taking a worn-away path which wound like a serpent before them, directed their course towards the east, where the sun was just then seen ascending above the mountain tops.

"When shall we get over the mountains, José?"

"By to-morrow evening, lieutenant, and from their summit—although too far off it is true—we shall perceive the end of our journey, that golden town of Mexico. Do you know what I am thinking of, lieutenant?"

Martinez did not reply.

"I ask myself what can have become of the officers of the ship and brig which we abandoned on the desert island."

Martinez trembled. "I do not know," he answered sullenly.

"I most heartily hope that all those great persons have died of hunger," continued José, "or perhaps when we landed them, some of them may have tumbled into the sea, and there is on those shores a kind of shark—the tintorea, who never lets anybody escape him. Holy Mary! should Captain Don Orteva have come to life he may have the chance of being swallowed up by a fish. But, happily, his head was struck by the mainboom, and by the noise it made must have been completely crushed."

"Hold your tongue!" replied Martinez.

The sailor rode on with closed mouth. "See what curious scruples this man has," said José to himself; he then added in his usual voice, "On my return I shall settle down in this charming country of Mexico, where one can enjoy, without stint, these beautiful ananas and bananas, and where one can eat off plates of gold and silver."

"Was it for this you mutinied?" asked Martinez.

"Why not, lieutenant? it was an affair of dollars."

"Ah!" exclaimed Martinez with disgust.

"And you, why did you mutiny?" inquired José.

"I! It was an affair of wounded honor. The lieutenant wished to be revenged on his captain."

"Ah!" exclaimed José with contempt.

There was not much difference between these two men whatever were their motives.

"Hold!" cried Martinez, pulling up short, "what do I see down there?"

José rode towards the edge of the cliff ."I can see no one," he replied.

"I saw a man suddenly disappear," repeated Martinez.

"Imagination!"

"I did see him," replied the lieutenant impatiently.

"Very well, look for him at your leisure," and José continued to ride on.

Martinez proceeded towards a clump of mangroves, the branches of which, taking root as they touched the ground, formed an impenetrable thicket. The lieutenant dismounted. It was a perfect solitude. Suddenly he perceived a spiral form moving about in the shade. It was a small species of serpent, the head held fast under a piece of rock, while the hinder part twisted about as if it had been galvanized.

"There has been someone here," cried the lieutenant. Guilty and superstitious, he looked around in every direction. He began to tremble. "Who, who can they be?" he murmured.

"Well! what is the matter?" asked José, who had now rejoined him.

"It is nothing," answered Martinez; "let us go on."

The evening approached. Martinez followed some paces

behind his guide José, and the latter, not without difficulty, found his way in the midst of the increasing darkness.

Looking out for a practicable path, swearing now at a stump against which he ran, now at the branch of a tree which struck him, threatening to put out the excellent cigar he was smoking, the lieutenant let his horse follow that of his companion. Useless remorse agitated him, and he gave himself up to the melancholy forebodings with which he was oppressed.

The night had now completely set in. The travelers pushed forward. They traversed without stopping, the little villages of Contepec and Iguala, and at length arrived at the town of Tasco. Here, little as they relished their food, their hunger was satisfied, and fatigue made even Martinez and José sleep until an hour after sunrise the next morning.

The lieutenant was the first to awake. " Let us start, Josê," he cried out.

The two Spaniards hastened to the stable, ordered their horses to be saddled, filled their saddle-bags with cakes of maize, grenadas, and dried meat, for among the mountains they would run a great risk of finding nothing to eat. The bill paid, they mounted their beasts and took the road once more.

" Have we nothing to fear among these solitudes? " asked Martinez.

" Nothing, excepting it may be a Mexican dagger! "

" That is true," answered Martinez, " the Indians of these elevated regions are still attached to the use of the dagger."

" Yes, indeed," replied the seaman, laughing. " What a number of words they have to designate their favorite arm—estoqe, verdugo, puna, anchillo, beldoque, navaja. The names come as quickly to their lips as the dagger does to their hands. Very well! so much the better. Holy Mary! at least we shall not have to fear those invisible balls from long carbines. I do not know anything more provoking than not to be able to discover the wretch who has killed one! "

" Who are the Indians who inhabit these mountains? " asked Martinez.

" Indeed, lieutenant, who can count the different races which have multiplied so rapidly in this El Dorado of Mexico? Just consider the various crosses, which I have studied carefully, with the intention of some day making an advantageous marriage. We here find the Mestisa, born of a Spaniard and an Indian woman; the Castisa, of a Castilian woman and a Spaniard; the Mulatto, of a Spanish woman and a Negro; the Monisque, born of a Mulatto woman and a Spaniard; the Albino, of a Monisque woman and a Spaniard; the Tintinclaire, of a Tornatras man and a Spanish woman; the Lovo, born of an Indian woman and a Negro; the Caribujo, of an Indian woman and a Lovo; the Barsino, born of a Coyote and a Mulatto woman; the Grifo, born of a Negress and a Lovo; the Albarazado, born of a Coyote and an Indian woman; the Chanesa, born of a Métis and an Indian man; the Mechino, born of a Lovo and a Coyote!"

José spoke the truth; the mixture of races in this country causes wonderful difficulties to anthropological students. Notwithstanding this learned conversation of the seaman, Martinez continually fell again into his previous taciturnity; he indeed sometimes pushed on ahead of his companion, whose presence seemed to annoy him.

In a short time two torrents crossed the road before them. The lieutenant pulled up at the first, disappointed on seeing that its bed was dry, for he had reckoned on watering his horse at it.

"Here we are, in a fix, lieutenant, without food and without water!" exclaimed José. "Never mind; follow me. We will look among these rocks and cliffs for the tree which is called the 'ahuehuelt,' which advantageously takes the place of the wisps of straw which decorate the fronts of inns. Under its shade one can always enjoy a cool draught, and, in a word, it is not only what some call water, but it is the wine of the desert."

The horsemen hunted about, and before long discovered the tree in question, but the promised fountain had been emptied, and they discovered it must have been visited only a short time previously.

"It is singular," observed José.

"It is indeed *singular*," said Martinez, growing pale. "Let us push forward."

The country now assumed an extremely rugged aspect. Gigantic peaks rose up before them, their basaltic summits stopping the clouds wafted by the winds from the Pacific.

Doubling a large rock there appeared high above them the Fort of Cochicalcho, built by the ancient Mexicans on a spot elevated nineteen thousand feet above the sea. The travelers directed their course towards the base of this vast cone, which was crowned by tottering rocks and crumbling ruins.

After having dismounted and fastened their horses to the trunk of a tree, Martinez and José, wishing to ascertain the direction of their road, climbed up to the summit of the cone, assisted by the ruggedness of the sides.

Night now coming on made the outline of objects appear very indistinct, and assume the most fantastic forms. The old fort did not ill-resemble an enormous bison, crouching down, its head immovable; but as Martinez looked at the figure, his disordered imagination made him fancy that he saw the body of the monstrous animal move. He did not, however, say anything lest he should lay himself open to the railleries of the unscrupulous José. The latter hastily made his way round a part of the hill, and after he had disappeared for some time behind some broken fragments, he summoned his companion with the loudness of his " Saint Iagos! " and " Saint Marias! "

All of a sudden, an enormous night-bird, uttering a hoarse shriek, slowly rose on its outstretched wings.

Martinez stopped short; a vast mass of rock was seen to shake about thirty feet above him, then a portion of the mass became detached, and, shattering everything in its passage with the rapidity of a cannon-ball, came crashing downwards, and was engulfed in the abyss below.

" Santa Maria! " cried the seaman. " Hello, lieutenant, what has happened? "

" José! "

" Here! " The two Spaniards joined each other.

" What a fearful avalanche descended on us! " exclaimed the seaman. Martinez followed him without saying a word, and the two soon regained the lower plateau.

Here a large furrow marked the passage of the rock.

" Santa Maria! " exclaimed José. " Look here! Our two horses have disappeared—crushed dead! "

" It is too true! " said Martinez.

" See here! " The tree to which the two animals had been fastened had been indeed carried away with them.

"If we had been under it!" philosophically observed the seaman, with a shrug of his shoulder.

Martinez was seized with a violent feeling of terror. "The serpent!—the fountain!—the avalanche!" he murmured.

Then he turned his haggard eyes on José.

"How is it that you do not speak to me of Captain Orteva?" he cried, his lips contracted with anger.

José drew back. "Oh, do not talk nonsense, lieutenant! Let us give the finishing stroke to our poor steeds and then push on. It will not do to stop here while the old mountain is combing her hair."

The two Spaniards proceeded on their road without saying a word, and in the middle of the night they arrived at Cuernavaca; but it was impossible to procure horses, so the next morning they directed their course on foot towards the heights of Popocatepetl.

CHAPTER IV
FROM CUERNAVACA TO POPOCATEPETL

THE temperature was cold and the country was devoid of vegetation. These inaccessible heights belonged to the icy zones, known as the cold territory. Already the fir trees of the foggy regions showed their withered outlines among the last oaks of these lofty elevations, and springs became more and more rare among the rugged rocks, consisting chiefly of porphyry and granite.

After six long hours the lieutenant and his companion began to drag themselves forward with difficulty, tearing their hands against rough masses of rock, and cutting their feet on the sharp stones in their path. At length fatigue compelled them to sit down. José occupied himself in preparing something to eat "What a cursed idea not to have taken the ordinary road!" he murmured.

They both, however, hoped to find at Aracopistla—a village completely shut in among the mountains—the means of transport to enable them to reach the end of their journey. But, after all, they might deceive themselves, and meet with the same want of accommodation and hospitality which they had encountered at Cuernavaca. They must, however, at all events, get there.

The road was fearfully parched and dry; on every side
fathomless precipices were to be seen in the sides of the
mountains, and rocks appeared ready to fall on the heads of
the travelers. To regain the chief road it was necessary
to cross a portion of these muontains at a height of five
thousand four hundred feet, near a rock known by the Indians as the "smoking rock," for it still exhibited signs of
recent volcanic action. Dark chasms yawned on every side.
Since the last journey of the seaman José some fresh out-
breaks had completely changed the appearance of these
solitudes, so that he could not recognize them; thus he completely lost himself among the inaccessible cliffs. He stopped
to listen to some rumbling sounds which came issuing forth
here and there from the cliffs.

"I can do no more!" at length cried José, sinking to the
ground with fatigue.

"Push on!" cried Martinez with feverish impatience.
Some claps of thunder reverberated amid the gorges of
Popocatepetl. "Now may Satan take me, for I may count
myself among the lost souls!"

"Rise up and push on," roughly exclaimed Martinez.
He compelled José to get up, and the sailor stumbled for-
ward. "And not a human being to guide us," murmured
José.

"So much the better," observed the lieutenant gruffly as
he moved forward.

"You do not know, then, that every year a thousand
murders are committed in Mexico, and how many in the
environs nobody can calculate!" said José.

"So much the better," answered Martinez.

Large drops of rain began to fall on the rocks around
them, brightened by the last fading light in the sky.

"The points we lately saw so clearly around us, where
are they now?" asked the lieutenant.

"Mexico is on the left, Puebla on the right," replied
José, "if we could see anything, but nothing can now be
distinguished."

It became fearfully dark. "Before us should be the
mountain of Icetacihualt, and in the ravine at its base a good
road; but what if we should not reach it!"

"Push on!" cried the lieutenant.

The thunder claps were now repeated with extreme

violence among the mountains. The rain and the wind, which had hitherto been silent, increased the loudness of the echoes. José went swearing on at every step. Lieutenant Martinez, pale and silent, gazed with sinister looks at his companion, whom he regarded as an accomplice he would gladly get rid of.

Suddenly a flash of lightning illuminated the obscurity. The seaman and the lieutenant were on the edge of an abyss.

Martinez hurried up to José, and after the last clap of thunder he said to him, "José, I am afraid!"

"Do you dread the storm?"

"I do not dread the storm in the sky, José; but I fear the storm which agitates my breast!"

"Oh, you are still thinking of Don Orteva! Come on, lieutenant! you make me laugh," answered José. He, however, did not laugh, as Martinez surveyed him with his haggard eyes.

A terrible clap of thunder burst over them.

"Hold your tongue! hold your tongue!" cried Martinez, who appeared to be no longer master of himself.

"The night is a favorable one for preaching to me!" replied the seaman. "If you have any fear, lieutenant, shut up your eyes and your ears."

"It seems to me," cried Martinez, "that I see the captain —Don Orteva—with his head crushed—there, there!"

A dark shadow, illuminated the next moment by a flash of lightning, arose within twenty feet of the lieutenant and his companion.

At the same instant José saw close to him Martinez, his countenance pale and distorted with passion, his hand grasping a dagger.

"What is there!" he cried out.

A flash of lightning environed them both.

"What! Kill me!" cried José. The next moment he fell, a corpse, and Martinez fled in the midst of the tempest, his bloody weapon in his hand.

A few moments afterwards two men hung over the dead body of the seaman, saying, "This is one of them!"

Martinez fled like a madman across the dark solitudes; his head uncovered, regardless of the rain, which came down in torrents.

"Kill! kill!" he shrieked out, stumbling over the slippery rocks.

Suddenly he heard a hoarse sound in the depths beneath his feet.   He stopped, knowing that it was the roaring of a torrent.

It was the little river Ixtolucca, which rushed on five hundred feet below him.   Some paces off, over the torrent, was thrown a bridge formed of ropes.   It was secured on both sides by some piles driven into the rock.   The bridge oscillated in the wind like a thread extended in space.

Clinging to the ropes, Martinez made his way across the bridge, and by a great effort he reached the opposite bank.

There, a shadow rose before him.

Martinez retreated, without saying a word, towards the bank he had just left.

There, another human form appeared.

Martinez fell upon his knees in the middle of the bridge, his hands clasped in despair.

"Martinez, I am Pablo!" said a voice.

"Martinez, I am Jacopo!" said another voice.

"You are a traitor!   You shall die!"

"You are a murderer!   You shall die!"

Two loud blows were heard, the piles which secured the ropes at the extremity of the bridge fell beneath the ax.   A horrible shriek rent the air, and Martinez, his hands extended, was precipitated into the abyss.

A league higher up, the midshipman and the boatswain rejoined each other, after having passed by a ford the river Ixtolucca.

"I have avenged Don Orteva!" said Jacopo.

"And I," replied Pablo, "have avenged Spain!"

It was thus that the navy of the Mexican Confederation had its origin.   The two Spanish ships, delivered up by the traitors, were taken possession of by the new Republic, and became the nucleus of that small fleet which fought unsuccessfully for Texas and California, against the fleet of the United States of America.

THE END.